## countless book bloggers h
## j.s. cooper's *ILLUSION*

"I loved the unique plot and the mystery woven into the storyline . . ."
—Harlequin Junkies

"Bianca and Jakob have stolen a piece of my heart . . ."
—A Bookish Escape

"The end of this book will answer a lot of questions, and then create new ones. . . . Also, it's worth noting that this is a trilogy, so I guess I'll be getting some anxiety meds."
—After Dark Book Lovers

"A cold shower is necessary (need I say more?). Some books should come with a warning—make sure your significant other is handy or your shower is in working order."
—Seduced by a Book

"*Illusion* is loaded with red-hot sexual tension, a budding romance that will make you swoon, and . . . J.S. Cooper has a gift of building a mystery that is unpredictable."
—Smut Books Junkie

"*Illusion* is the book readers are calling a roller-coaster ride of emotions. It's achingly sexy, steaming hot, full of romance, and has suspense that will keep you guessing until the last page . . . It had me on the edge of my seat."
—Smokin' Hot Book Reviews

"The Swept Away series by J.S. Cooper is fervently romantic plus ingeniously mysterious."
—Sensual Reads

"OMG OMG OMG OMG!!! This book was AMAZING! . . . If you are looking for a book that is different than the rest of the cookie-cutter books out there and wanting something with some great action and mystery then this is the book for you! 5 Stars!"
—Turning Pages at Midnight

## by j.s. cooper and gallery books

## the swept away series

*Charade*

*Illusion*

## other bestselling series from j.s. cooper

*The Ex Games*

*The Ex Games 2*

*The Ex Games 3*

*After the Ex Games*

*The Private Club*

*The Private Club 2*

*The Private Club 3*

# disillusioned

j.s. cooper

G

GALLERY BOOKS

New York London Toronto Sydney New Delhi

G

Gallery Books
An Imprint of Simon & Schuster, Inc.
1230 Avenue of the Americas
New York, NY 10020

This book is a work of fiction. Any references to historical events, real people, or real places are used fictitiously. Other names, characters, places, and events are products of the author's imagination, and any resemblance to actual events or places or persons, living or dead, is entirely coincidental.



First Gallery Books trade paperback edition March 2015

GALLERY BOOKS and colophon are registered trademarks of Simon & Schuster, Inc.

For information about special discounts for bulk purchases, please contact Simon & Schuster Special Sales at 1-866-506-1949 or business@simonandschuster.com.

The Simon & Schuster Speakers Bureau can bring authors to your live event. For more information or to book an event, contact the Simon & Schuster Speakers Bureau at 1-866-248-3049 or visit our website at www.simonspeakers.com.

Manufactured in the United States of America

10 9 8 7 6 5 4 3 2 1

Library of Congress Cataloging-in-Publication Data

Cooper, J. S.
Disillusioned / J.S. Cooper.—First Gallery Books trade paperback edition.
pages ; cm.—(Swept away ; 2)
1. Castaways—Fiction. 2. Man-woman relationships—Fiction. I. Title.
PS3603.O582637D57 2015
813'.6—dc23 2014045403

ISBN 978-1-4767-9099-2
ISBN 978-1-4767-9104-3 (ebook)

*To the stars. There are no more clouds.*

# acknowledgments

This book was a labor of love. Thank you to Tanya Kay Skaggs, Katrina Jaekley, Stacy Hahn, Tianna Croy, Cilicia White, Kathy Corbett Shreve, and Gillian Hedges for your excitement as you read this book chapter by chapter. Thank you to all the J.S. Cooper Indie Agents and readers for your overwhelming support of my work. Thank you to my editor, Abby Zidle, for pointing out errors and mistakes in a way that doesn't make me feel like I failed the human race. Thank you to my agent, Rebecca Friedman, for always being there to offer a listening ear and to providing feedback that is always helpful. Thank you to my good friend Emily Fauquet for driving me to Barnes & Noble so that I could see and buy *Illusion* in a bookstore. Thank you to Violeta Bermudez-Estrella for making me take a photo with the *Illusion* paperback after I bought it and posting it all over Instagram. Thank you to all the readers that sent me messages excited to see a book of mine in a bookstore. Your excitement and my excitement were one and the same. Thank you to Katherine Brown for being my biggest supporter from my hot-prof blogging days to now. I can still remember live blogging *Grey's Anatomy* every week knowing you were going to read it and comment. And I was just as excited to have one reader as I am to have many more now. Thanks to my mum for finally buying two copies of *Illusion* after I begged you several times to look for the book in the bookstore. It doesn't matter if I have a copy at home, you still need to buy it, mum! And as always, thanks be to God for all of His blessings.

# prologue

The moment the world changed colors all seems like a dream now. I always think back to that moment and it always plays back slightly differently in my head. You'd think I'd have remembered every single word and action from that day, but I don't. Each kiss and each sentence is muddled in my mind and the replay is always unique, however, I will never forget the way that I felt.

"Did you really think I'd let you go, Bianca?" His voice sounded muffled as he whispered in my ear softly through the material that was tied around my eyes and across my ears. "Did you think I'd just give up?" The tip of his tongue trailed from the inside of my ear and down the side of my neck. I shivered in the cool room as I strained to move my hands. The rope was tight around my wrists and I struggled in the bed.

"Why are you doing this, Mattias?" I said as his lips pressed against mine roughly.

"Because you want me to." He bit down on my lower

lip and tugged gently. “And because I want to.” He leaned down closer to me and I breathed in his scent, wallowing in the smell of his cologne. The first time I’d smelled him I’d instinctively been attracted to him. I could still remember being in the back of the dark car with him the night I’d been kidnapped. My eyes felt heavy as I thought about his betrayal. How could Jakob have done this to me? How could I have not known he was Mattias?

“You need to trust me, Bianca.” His voice was monotone as he kissed me again, and I tried to avoid breathing in his smell.

“You said that last time,” I whispered, and my body froze as I smelled him again. This time every nerve in my body tingled with shock as the bold musk of the familiar cologne hit me, sending shock waves through my body. His kiss was searching and demanding; wanting something that had been forbidden to him. I lay there, unmoving, trying not to betray my fear.

“I want to make you mine, Bianca. We can make this work.” His voice deepened and I tried not to cringe as I felt his fingers in my hair. I remained tight-lipped, scared that my voice would give something away.

“No,” I said softly, and he froze, confirming what I already knew. “I know who you are.” This time my voice was stronger.

“That’s why this will be so very enjoyable, Bianca,” he muttered, and kissed my cheek before stepping back. “Let the games begin.”

# one

### One Week Earlier

"Bianca, open up!" I could hear Jakob's voice through the open window. My heart broke at the sound of worry in his tone. At one time, I would have believed that the concern was for me and my well-being. Now I knew better. Now I knew all Jakob cared about was finding out what I knew and scaring me into trusting him. My body shivered as the cool ocean breeze washed over my trembling skin. I held on to the railing of the balcony and said a quick prayer before I prepared to jump to the next one. It was only a couple of yards away, but I just knew that those couple of yards of space were waiting to pull me down like a dead weight. I looked down at the drop between the two balconies and sank to the floor in fear, unable to take the leap.

"Bianca!" Jakob's voice was louder as I heard a loud crack coming from inside the bathroom. Adrenaline kicked in—I forced myself to my feet and over the rail at last. "Bianca, stop," he shouted at me as he poked his head out of the bathroom window.

"One, two, three. You got this." I took a deep breath and jumped. My ankle caught the railing and I screamed as I landed with a thud on the balcony of the next room.

"Bianca, are you okay?" His silky tone almost deceived me as I struggled to get up. I heard him walking onto the balcony I'd just left, and I scrambled to open the sliding door that led to the bedroom. The lights were off and my heart was beating fast as I tried to open the door.

"Open, please, open." I bit my lower lip as I tugged frantically on the handle.

"Bianca, please, don't make me come over there."

"Don't even think about it!" I shouted as I turned to look at him.

His blue eyes were focused on my face as he stood a mere couple of yards away. "You can't get in there." He shook his head. "The door's locked and the room is vacant."

"How do you know that?"

"I made sure of that fact when we arrived." He shrugged. "I didn't want us to have any distractions."

"You mean you didn't want me to find out the truth!" I shouted, anger making me brave. I stared at his profile as he looked at something in the distance. His face looked so familiar, so ruggedly handsome, so much like that of the Jakob I'd come to have feelings for that my heart broke when he turned to look back at me.

“Why are you running from me, Bianca?”

“Do you think I’m crazy?” I shook my head and tightened the bathrobe belt around my waist. “Do you think I’d stay with you after what I heard?”

“What do you think you heard, Bianca?”

“What do I *think* I heard?” I repeated. “Help me, somebody help me!” I screamed into the night air, hoping a passing stranger or another hotel guest might hear my cries.

“Bianca, calm down.” He grimaced as he stared at me. “Take some deep breaths and stop panicking. Let your common sense control the situation, not your fear.”

“What?” My eyes narrowed as I stared at him, my heart racing fast.

“I was on a deserted island with you, Bianca. I know how your mind works.”

“It’s a pity I don’t know how your mind works, *Jakob*,” I said sarcastically, my fear dissipating as I stared at him. He wouldn’t hurt me, would he? He hadn’t hurt me on the island. He hadn’t done anything to make me scared of him. I had to believe that he wasn’t looking to hurt me now. But I couldn’t fathom how I’d given myself to this man. I’d made love to him. I’d trusted him. I could feel hysteria bubbling to the surface as I stared at his naked chest, muscular and toned in the moonlight. Laughter erupted, flowing out of me with abandon, sounding manic and crazy in the still night.

“Bianca?” His eyes narrowed and his face looked worried as I continued laughing.

"That's my name, *Jakob*," I said eventually, after my laughter had subsided and all that was left was a dry throat and a heavy heart.

"What is it you think you know?" He leaned over and I stepped back.

"I don't think I know. I know that I know." I glared at him, the anger in me giving me the strength to face him. "I heard you speaking to that man. You told him that Steve deviated from the plan. What plan is that, huh? We were on an island with a crazy man that both of us didn't know. Now I know that's not the truth. Now I know that we weren't both kidnapped. You weren't there as an innocent bystander with me, were you?" My voice caught as the depths of his deviousness hit me fully. "You could have killed me. I don't even know you. I don't know what you're capable of . . . if you could kidnap me and lie to my face, what else could you do?"

"I would never hurt you, Bianca. You have to believe that. That's not who I am." His voice was filled with emotion as he gazed at me, a calm look on his face. How could he be so cool, when everything was crumbling around him? All his lies were coming out now.

"Why did you lie to me?" My voice trembled as I stared at the man I'd just spent a week with, believing that he'd been kidnapped as well. "You knew Steve." I bit my lower lip as the enormity of that statement hit me. "You knew he didn't just *happen* to be lost on the same island. You sent him there to be with us. You *planned* this."

"You think I planned your kidnapping and my own?" The surprise in the way he said the words made me feel ridiculous, but I knew what I'd heard.

"And I spoke to David and—well, you're Mattias, aren't you?" My voice dropped and I looked out at the night sky. I could see the waves of the ocean crashing against the rocks from where I was standing. The blackness of the sky was illuminated by a million radiant white stars. The setting was as romantic as it could be, yet I felt no appreciation for its beauty.

"You think I'm Mattias?" he asked simply.

I looked into his eyes, seeking out an answer in his dark pupils. "Well, aren't you? Mattias went to such lengths to avoid me when I was dating his brother—obviously you wanted to keep your identity a secret since you were planning to abduct me."

"You think Mattias is bad?" He took a small step forward on his balcony.

"I think *you're* bad, yes."

His eyes crinkled then and I saw them narrow for a second before he looked away and mumbled something to himself.

"What did you say?" I asked, unable to stop myself.

"You make this so goddamn hard, Bianca," he growled. I swallowed nervously. I could see his nostrils flaring as the breeze sent another chill down my spine. My eyes involuntarily fell to his crotch, and when I looked back up, a half smile was on his face. "I didn't say me."

"What?" I blushed, looking away from him, an inner

heat warming me involuntarily. I stared at some palm trees a couple hundred yards away. They were swaying back and forth and I watched as a coconut fell to the ground.

"I said this situation was hard, not me." His voice was soft and provocative, trying to lure me back to him.

"I never said you were hard." I looked back at him, my nerve almost failing when I looked into his eyes and saw the gentle, teasing Jakob I had gotten to know on the island.

"But you were hoping I was, weren't you?" he teased me again and stepped forward. My heart stopped as he grabbed a hold of the railing in front of him.

"Don't come over here," I whispered, my voice cracking. "Please."

"Why are you scared of me, Bianca? You know I would never hurt you." His eyes looked sad and I wondered at his being such a great actor. It was almost ironic, with me being a movie critic. I'd witnessed the greatest performance live and in person, but I hadn't even known I was being played.

"How could you make love to me?" My voice dropped and my legs tingled as I thought about the way he had kissed and caressed me just minutes before. My skin felt warm as I remembered the things he had done with his tongue, and I sighed as my body betrayed me. *Trust him*, it said. *Let him hold you and keep you warm.* I closed my eyes and took a couple of deep breaths. I needed to focus. I was like Julia Roberts in *Sleeping with the Enemy*. I needed to be on high alert. I couldn't allow him to twist the truth and turn me against myself.

"I made love to you because you're beautiful. I made love to you because I couldn't not make love to you. In fact, I want to make love to you right now." He smiled and then looked at my chest suggestively. "Come, dear Bianca, let's just go back to bed."

"Just tell me two things." I spoke confidently and felt a surge of pride running through my veins as I hid my fear. "Did you know Steve before he showed up on the island with us? And were you really kidnapped?" I waited for his answers, the events of the last week flashing through my mind like a movie on fast-forward.

It felt as if just yesterday I was sitting in the bar with my best friend, Rosie, having a glass of wine. She'd gone to the bathroom and I'd blacked out. The next thing I'd known I was in the back of a car tied up with a strange man. A man who'd turned out to be Jakob. I hadn't trusted him at first, but he had slowly proven himself to me, and I hadn't been able to resist my attraction to him. Together we'd worked to figure out why we'd been kidnapped. That was what I'd believed in my heart. We'd both talked about our personal histories. I'd told him about my dad's death and how I'd thought the rich Bradley family had had something to do with my mother's death. He'd told me about his mother and her heartache when the man she'd loved hadn't committed to her. And when Steve had showed up—nefarious, deceitful, smarmy Steve—I'd seen the surprise, shock, and distaste on Jakob's face.

I thought we'd connected on a deeper level. I'd given

myself to him, mind, body, and heart. I'd put my trust and faith in him. Could he have been fooling me all of this time? Could he have done this to me in the first place?

"Bianca, it's complicated." He bit his lower lip and his eyes narrowed again. I could see his tension in the way his shoulders were hunched up. His fists were clenched and I could see a vein throbbing in his forehead.

I took a step toward him, feeling brave in pursuit of the truth. "Why so worried? Angry that I know the truth?"

"What truth do you think you know?" He threw his hands up, and I could see his palms were still roughened from his time on the island cracking coconuts and carrying wood. "You need to trust me," he pleaded.

"How can I trust you? You lied to me and even now you're not telling me anything."

"What you think you know about Mattias—well, it's complicated."

"You mean what I think I know about *you*?"

"It's complicated, Bianca. You need to just trust me for now, please."

"Did you have any involvement with my kidnapping?" I asked softly, and stared at him, our chests rising in unison as we stood mere yards away from one another.

"Give me your hand," he said softly, and stretched his arms as forward as they could go.

"Why?" I shook my head, but didn't step back. I suppose I was waiting for an answer that would make everything clearer. Something that would show me Jakob wasn't involved in this whole mess.

"Please."

I found myself reaching my hand forward slowly. I regretted my decision about a second later.

His fingers squeezed mine tightly and I gasped at the dart of pain that surged through me at his tight grip. "I'm sorry," he whispered as he stared at me from the other balcony. "I didn't mean to hurt you, Bianca."

"Then let go of me." I tried to pull it away from him again, but he wouldn't release me. "Please."

"Bianca." His voice was hoarse. "I can't let you go."

"Why did you lie to me?" I shook my head and stared into his eyes. For a few seconds we were back on the island. For a few seconds it was just us against the world. For a few seconds my heart stopped beating and I was caught up in the magnetism that attracted us to each other. As I stared into his deep blue eyes, I felt a gamut of emotions: pain, anger, sadness, and something akin to love. My heart broke as I saw the same emotions reflected back at me.

"Bianca."

"My name is not an answer," I grated out.

"Just trust me." His eyes bore into mine as our fingers held on to each other. My body wanted to believe him with everything that I had, but my brain was being smarter this time.

"That's not an answer either."

"What do I need to do for you to trust me?"

"Let me go," I pleaded.

"That's not safe." He shook his head.

"I don't feel safe being here with you."

"It wasn't supposed to be like this." His fingers dug into my skin. "I didn't count on this, Bianca."

"You didn't answer my questions. Did you know Steve and were you kidnapped?"

"You know the answers," he said simply, his eyes never leaving mine.

"Is David your brother?" I asked softly, not even allowing myself to breathe as I waited for his answer. *Please say no, please say no, please say no.* Even as I expected the answer, I prayed he wasn't my ex-boyfriend's reclusive brother, Mattias.

"Yes." He nodded. "Yes, David is my brother."

I was distracted then by a sudden movement on the ground below us. A group of people walked toward the hotel down a narrow pathway.

"Help!" I screamed. "Help me!" I yanked my hand away and tumbled to the floor. "Help!" I screamed again, needing them to hear me, but as they looked around in confusion, a bird flew past them and distracted them, and my faint cry was forgotten.

"Bianca, stop it!"

"Leave me alone!" I wanted him to know that I wouldn't be silenced.

"Bianca, we had something special. Please, give me the chance to explain."

"We had *nothing*," I spat. "It means *nothing*. You ruined it all with your lies." Tears ran down my face as in shock I made the transition from anger to complete and utter devastation.

"I'm coming over." Jakob stood on the top of the balcony railing, balancing like an acrobat before getting ready to jump over, and I felt myself stilling as he stood there.

"Get down." My heart was in my throat as he balanced without moving. "You could fall."

"So you still care." He gave me a satisfied smile as he stepped back onto his balcony.

"Why didn't you come over here?" I was confused. He could easily have grabbed me if he wanted to. All he had to do was make one small jump. Why hadn't he?

"Have you ever seen *The Talented Mr. Ripley*, Bianca?"

"The movie with Matt Damon and Jude Law?" I frowned at his randomness. Why was he bringing up movies? That was my thing. "Yes, a long time ago. Why?"

"I want you to trust me, Bianca. Everything isn't as it seems."

"Yeah, you're not as you seem, *Jakob*." I paused. "Jakob Bradley, right?"

"My last name is Bradley." He nodded solemnly. "It's not a name I carry with pride."

"I wonder why." I glared at him. "I assume you hate it as much as you hate your first name."

"Life is complicated, Bianca. Sometimes we have to make decisions we don't want to make. It's just what life brings us."

"Like when Ripley kills Peter at the end of the movie?"

"Ripley loved Peter." Jakob sighed. "But he had to do what he had to do."

"Are you telling me you have to kill me?"

"I would never harm you."

"What do you want from me?"

"I want the same thing you want, Bianca." His face changed and he looked away. "We've both come so far."

"Do you want me to cede my father's patents to Bradley Inc.? Is that what this is about?" I asked bitterly. "Is this what everything has been about? Your family screwed my father over and stole his inventions. Now that he's passed away, you're worried that I'll take your family to court. If I win, you'll have to give me a huge share in the company and that will give your family a bad name."

"This is about more than that, Bianca. There are things you don't know about those patents. I don't care, but . . ." His voice trailed off as he stretched his arms up and I could hear the tiredness I felt reflected in his voice. "You haven't been totally truthful with me either."

"What are you talking about?"

"I know about the other letters."

"What?" I frowned as I stared at him in shock. "What do you mean?"

"I know the secrets you're hiding. I know what your father did. I know the truth behind his guilt."

"My father felt guilty because my mother died and he

didn't put the pieces together soon enough to get justice for her death."

"Do you really think that's the only reason he was upset, Bianca?" Jakob's eyes searched mine. "Are you seriously trying to tell me you didn't know about the affair?"

"What?" My jaw dropped as I gazed at him, my mind racing. With that one word, everything I thought I knew was called into question. I remembered the label on the box that had held my father's papers. It had read "divorce papers." I hadn't thought much of it when I'd seen it. I figured it was a box from one of Larry's old clients, but maybe it wasn't. Maybe it was a box that had held divorce papers for my parents. Maybe they hadn't been as happy as I'd thought they'd been. Had there really been an affair? My stomach dropped as a surge of pain ran through my veins. I didn't want to believe that either of my parents could have stepped outside of the marriage.

All of a sudden Jakob was on my balcony, grabbing my hands and pulling me toward him. "Don't run away again, Bianca." His eyes looked dark as he gazed down on me. "It's not safe here."

"But aren't you the one I should be afraid of?" I whispered up at him as he leaned down to kiss me roughly.

# two

His lips, though rough, felt like heaven against my lips as my body melted into him, momentarily forgetting how much I hated him. His fingers gripped my hips possessively as he pulled me into him and thrust his hardness into my stomach. My stomach churned as I pulled away from him, my mind battling with my heart.

"Don't," I said urgently as my hands pushed against his chest.

"Why, Bianca, why?" he growled as he bit down on my lips. "Why did you have to be her, Bianca? Why couldn't it have been anyone but you?"

"What do you mean?"

"You're a good liar, aren't you?" He stepped back and his arms fell away from me, leaving me feeling bereft. He eyes searched my face and I shivered. "Or did you really not know?"

"I'm not the liar." I was taken aback and confused by his words. "Did I really not know what?"

“You nearly caught me in your trap, but I suppose that was your plan, wasn’t it?”

“What plan, Jak—Matt . . . ?” I sputtered in confusion, no longer sure what to call him. Jakob felt wrong, but Mattias felt too twisted—and too real.

“You’re just like your mother—beautiful, angelic, and calculating.” He shook his head, his eyes narrowing as he surveyed me in disgust. “Though I wonder if she was as good an actress as you are.”

“I’m not an actress.” I stared at him, wondering how he had turned this around on me. I was pretty sure that was the sign of a sociopath. Apparently he was a pretty talented one, because all I could think about was what he had said about my mother. Was she somehow involved in this? As more than an innocent bystander?

“I wouldn’t expect you to say anything else.”

“It’s a bit like the pot calling the kettle black, isn’t it?” I was angry as I stared at him. “How convenient for you to place the lies on me.”

“I’m sorry.” He sighed heavily. “I didn’t want to take this out on you, like this.” He rubbed his temple. “I’ve just thought about this for so long, not this moment, but your mother and what she did to my family.”

“My mother didn’t do anything to your family, Jakob.”

“My mother lost the man she loved because of your mom.” His voice was hollow as he gazed at me. “I know you’re not your mom. I know that I shouldn’t blame you for her sins, but I just don’t know what to think.”

"Think about what?" I said angrily. "I'm the one that gets to be mad at you, Jakob. You're the one that lied to me, not the other way around."

"I feel guilty." His voice was hoarse and pained. "I fell for you in a very deep and real way. I want you to trust me, but a part of me wonders if this wasn't what your mom did as well. Was this how she stole my father away? Did she have the same angelic face and beguiling eyes? Did she trap my father with her casual innocence and aura of sex?"

"My mother didn't do anything." My voice was thin. "This situation is about you and how you lied to me. This is about how you kidnapped me and tricked me."

"Just answer me one question, Bianca." He took a step back and surveyed my face, his eyes keen and aware. I waited for him to ask his question. What could he possibly want to know that would make this any better for him?

"What?"

"Do you truly believe your parents were perfect? Do you really think their marriage was ruined only by death?"

"That's two questions." I was affronted. Of course my parents' marriage had been perfect. I could still remember how devastated my father had been when my mother died. He'd loved her so much. They'd been a perfect couple, the couple that we all aspired to be.

I was about to answer when all of a sudden a memory hit me: I was sitting on the floor in the corner of a room, playing with two stuffed toys while my parents were whispering furiously. I looked up to the side to see tears streaming down my mother's face. My father was gripping her arms tightly and muttering something indecipherable. I sat there playing with my toys and turned away from my parents, oblivious of the tension in the air. I closed my eyes and tried to focus on the memory.

What had they been arguing about? I was pretty sure I could remember my mother saying, "I didn't love him," but then the memory changed to my father's voice saying, "I didn't love her." My eyes popped open and I stared into Jakob's astute eyes. I could feel the blood draining from my face as I stood there, my body cold in the warm night. What memory was that, then? I started to shiver as I pictured my mom's tears and sobs. Had she cheated on my father?

"I see that you understand now." His voice was cold.

"Understand what?" I whispered, not blinking for fear of my tears falling and embarrassing me. I felt numb inside, and only part of that feeling stemmed from the truth I'd found out about Jakob's being David's brother and a Bradley.

"That there's more to this story than just your innocent mother dying." Jakob's voice was emotionless. "There's more to this story than you think you—"

"Yes, there's more to this story. I want to know if your father had my mother killed. I want to know if you've been keeping it a secret. I want to know why you had me kidnapped. I want to take you down, Mattias Bradley! I want to take you and your entire family down."

"You don't know . . . ?" He paused as he looked at me, his eyes never leaving mine, and I could see that he was waging a battle in his mind.

"What don't I know?"

"You really don't know about your mother, do you?" He sighed. "Your parents, like most parents, weren't perfect, Bianca."

"What are you trying to say?" I asked softly. "What are you intimating, Jakob?"

"I think your mother deliberately seduced my father," he said softly. "Your mother ruined my mother's relationship with my father and that ruined my mother's life."

"No." The blood drained from my face. "My mother wouldn't do that. She loved my father. They were in love. You must be mistaken."

"I don't think so." He looked tense. "I'm searching for the truth as well, Bianca. That's what we both want, right? The truth?"

I nodded.

"Bianca," he said softly, his voice cracking. "Don't you feel this?" He put his hands up in the air and I could see his fingers trembling slightly.

"Feel what?"

"This moment. This is hard for both of us because of our feelings for each other."

"I don't have feelings for you," I said quickly.

"Liar," he whispered, and turned to look at the ocean. I stared at his profile as he stood there, lost in thought.

"No, I think that's you, Jakob—or Mattias Bradley."

He turned to look back at me. This time his blue eyes were calm, the storm inside his head having passed.

"I need you to trust me, Bianca. I can't tell you everything you want to know. Not yet. I need to figure some things out first. And I need to make sure you're safe."

"I'll be safe if I'm away from you."

"I don't think so." He sighed. "Look, I knew Steve, and, yes, I asked him to come to the island. That was a part of the plan. He was meant to scare you so that I could protect you and we'd get closer."

"Oh." I stepped back, my hand flying to my mouth as I realized how perfectly Jakob's plan had worked.

"He deviated from the plan, Bianca." Jakob took another step toward me, and I held up my hand for him to stop. I was surprised when he stood still. "I need to figure out why. I need to know who got to him and what his purpose was for turning on me."

"So ask him."

"He's gone." Jakob ran his hand across his head. "I don't know how or where, but he's gone. I don't want you to leave until I know. Please."

"If you have any chance of me ever trusting you, you will let me leave." My voice was as cold as the deepest ocean. "This isn't the island anymore." I looked around and took a deep breath. "I don't need your help and I don't want it. Let me go. If there is any part of you that regrets kidnapping me, let me go."

"We need to figure out the truth, Bianca."

"The truth is you kidnapped me. The truth is that you're a Bradley. That's all the truth I need from you right now."

He shook his head slowly and sighed. "You can leave in the morning. I'll have someone take you to the airport. A private plane will be waiting to take you back to New York."

"You're going to let me leave?" I was shocked that he'd taken in my words and changed his mind so quickly.

"What choice do I have?" He clenched his fists. "I was never going to physically hurt you."

"Well, your man Steve didn't seem to get the memo."

"I told you, Steve deviated from the plan." Jakob's gaze grew darker. "I will deal with him. I never had any plan to hurt you."

"Just to kidnap me, then?"

"I . . ." He took a deep breath. "I wanted some answers from you."

"What sort of answers?"

"I wanted to know about your parents' marriage."

"Why?"

"I needed to know if your parents were responsible for my father—"

"For your father what?" I cut him off, wanting everything to make sense. I wanted the pieces of the puzzle to fit together and leave me in peace. I wanted to go back to a normal life, to a time before I'd met Jakob. I didn't want to remember what it felt like to be with him: to be kissed by him, to be touched by him, to be filled with him. He had become such a part of me in such a short time, and I wasn't sure how to process all the information I had now. I didn't want to go down this path any further. I was scared to find out more information that I didn't want to know. I was scared that my parents' marriage wasn't as perfect as I remembered its being. "For your father leaving your mother?"

"It doesn't matter." His eyes narrowed. "I have other things to take care of first."

"What other things?"

"I need to find out who got to Steve and why . . ." His voice trailed off and he looked out to the ocean. "I suggest you leave well enough alone, Bianca."

"What's that supposed to mean?"

"Stop being Nancy Drew. Take this opportunity and disappear."

"You think I'm playing a part?"

"I don't even know what you're doing, Bianca." His lips thinned. "In other circumstances, I would have been curious. Now, I don't care."

"You don't care?" Hurt coursed through my veins.

"You tricked me once, Bianca. I won't let you trick me again."

"How did I trick you? What are you talking about?" My head was running in circles at his words. He was a master manipulator, that was for sure. He even had me questioning myself and my motives. He seemed genuinely confused as to why Steve had become more sinister. I was pretty confident that Jakob was legitimately perplexed as to why Steve had turned on him. Though, I didn't know if I was smart to trust my instincts. I'd already been wrong once.

"Let it go, Bianca." He sighed. "I can't let my feelings for you stop me from doing what I need to do."

"What do you need to do?"

"As much as you don't trust me, I don't know if I can trust you." He glanced at me for a few seconds again, and his eyes ran up and down my body, unable to hide his lust.

"Fine, then neither one of us trusts each other." I glared at him, my heart beating fast as he gazed at my legs.

"Come with me. Could we spend one more night together?" he asked softly, his tone smooth.

"What do you mean, come with you? Are you joking?" I shouted. "I'm not going anywhere with you!"

"This is confusing for me as well."

"I don't care what this is for you, you liar."

"Bianca—"

"Don't say my name!" I screamed.

"I wish I understood you." He seemed sad. "I wish I understood who you really are."

"I wish I knew who you really are as well, Jakob."

"We're like the mountain and the treacherous deep blue ocean," he said wryly.

"Why's that?"

"We're both powerful in our own ways and we both have hidden depths and dangers." All of a sudden he looked sad. "And you never see them next to each other."

"What do you mean?"

"Have you ever seen a mountain overlooking the ocean?"

"No, I've never seen that."

"I wish I could trust you, Bianca. I wish I could tell you the truth and know that you'd understand—"

"You wish *you* could trust *me*?" I laughed. "I will never trust you again, never."

"I wish you would." He grabbed my arms and pulled me to him. "Don't you understand, Bianca, this is more than both of us. This is about a past that neither one of us understands."

"What would you have me do, Jakob?" I asked softly. "What would you have me do?"

"Forget everything." His voice was tense as he pleaded with me. The muscles at the side of his jaw were clenched. "If you want to be safe, you need to forget everything."

"I don't care about being safe. I want answers. I want to know if my mother was murdered. I want to know if your father had her killed just so he could have a successful business."

"Do you think it's as simple as that, Bianca? Do you think that life is ever as simple as that?"

"You know the answers. You know secrets that I don't. And I don't know why you won't tell me." I gulped. "What are you afraid of, Jakob? Are you scared that I'm going to take all of your money? Are you afraid that this hotel, your planes, your cars, everything you own, is going to belong to me? Is that why you kidnapped me? Is that why you tried to frighten me off? At what point did you come up with this plan? Was it the first time that David asked you to meet me or the fifth? Is this why you never wanted us to meet?" I froze as thoughts ran in my head clumsily.

"David never told me you were anxious to meet . . ." Jakob frowned as his voice trailed off.

"Sure he didn't. I've been wanting to meet you for a long time, Mattias. You know that. David called you repeatedly while we were together, but you'd never accept our invitations. And meeting you—or should I say Mattias—was all I talked about on the island. Oh, how you must have laughed at me!"

"I never laughed at you."

"How gullible I was," I continued as if he hadn't spoken. "From the first moment, when I came to in the trunk of the car, you must have been laughing at me. How easy I was to fool."

"Bianca, what we had, what we shared, it was—"

"Shut up." I glared at him, my heart feeling as if it were going to explode in sadness and confusion. "Just shut up. I don't want to hear what you have to say. I don't want to listen to your lies anymore."

"Maybe the person you're maddest at is yourself."

"Why would I be mad at myself?" I snarled at him, but I knew that he was partially right. Even now a part of me wanted to trust him. I'd let my guard down when I had no idea who he really was. I had given myself to him. Even now my body craved his touch and wanted to go back to the hotel room with him. I wanted to be touched, consumed, taken, by him. I wanted to wake up from this nightmare that had become my life. I wanted him to be my Jakob, my protector, the man who'd made me believe there was someone out there for me. And that made me hate myself and my weakness for this man.

"Maybe because you ignored the true clues, the answers that were sitting right in front of you. Maybe you know what the truth really is and you just don't want to admit it to yourself."

"You have a gift." I shook my head sadly. "You have a gift for manipulating people. If I wasn't so strong, you might have made me believe this was all in my head, that I was the one in the wrong."

"The truth always wins out, Bianca." His eyes narrowed. "And we do pay for the sins of our fathers and mothers." He sighed. "But none of this is in your head, Bianca. We both know that. It just might be that we're on opposite sides of the truth."

"The opposite of the truth is falsehood," I said softly. "You're on the side of lies."

"It could be that we're both on the side of the truth. But that's something we still need to figure out. I just hope that I can do it soon."

"Let's hope so." I stared at him, wondering how I could both love and hate so deeply the man in front of me. "I certainly hope so."

# three

I didn't open my eyes until the plane landed in New York. I felt like a stranger to my own city as I stood in the taxi line with the small brown bag a nameless air steward had given me along with a wad of bills. I opened the bag slowly, wondering what Jakob had sent me home with. The bag contained my cell phone, a cardigan, an envelope, and a bottle of water. I stared at the items blankly, my mind still fuzzy from the plane ride. I couldn't believe I was finally back in civilization. I couldn't believe he had let me go, just like that. Why had he kidnapped me if he'd been so willing to let me go so easily? My heart felt heavy as I realized that the end had come before there had even been a beginning. I had already failed.

"Where you going, ma'am?" the taxi guy asked as the next yellow cab pulled up.

"Manhattan."

"Cross streets?"

"Sorry, what?"

"What's the address?" He sounded annoyed as he looked past me to the long line of people waiting.

"Oh." I bit my lower lip. "Forty-Second Street, Times Square."

"You wanna go to Times Square?"

"Yes." I nodded. That wasn't my address, but I didn't want to go directly home. I needed to be around lights and people. I needed to be anywhere but home right now.

"Okay, go up to that cab." He pointed a few cabs ahead and I walked up to the cab. I looked inside and froze as I saw Steve behind the wheel. My face grew red and my body grew heavy as I stood there.

"You going to Times Square?" the man said in a slightly accented voice, and I nodded and took a deep breath as I stared at the man's dark skin. This was not Steve. He was not Steve. I needed to stop freaking out.

"Yes, thanks."

"Back from vacation?" he asked conversationally as we pulled off.

"No."

"Work trip?"

"No."

I saw him peer in the rearview mirror. "You're not going to be sick, are you?" He frowned as he looked back ahead at the traffic, the mirror showing his furtive glances back at me.

"No, I'm not."

"Good." He pulled into traffic. "I don't want to clean up any—"

"I'm not going to be sick," I snapped, wanting him to shut up. I opened the bag again and turned on my phone. The battery was fully charged and I waited for my texts and voice mails to come through. I was positive that I was going to have millions of texts from Rosie. She must have been so worried about me. I waited for the phone to download all my messages and called my voice mail. I was surprised to hear, "You have two new voice mails." Only two? That was weird. I pressed one to hear the first voice mail.

"Bianca." Rosie's voice was loud and I could hear music in the background. "The bartender told me that you left with some guy. I can't believe you didn't even tell me bye. Call me tomorrow with all the details. I can't wait to hear about your wild night. Love you." Then she hung up. I frowned as I realized that someone had told Rosie that I'd left with someone. Did she not even realize that I hadn't been in town for weeks? But looking back, I realized that it hadn't been weeks or months. It felt like a lifetime, but had only been about a week and a half, if that. Time had lost all meaning on the island. I pressed SAVE and then listened to the second voice mail.

"Bianca, it's Larry. I think we should talk. Give me a call when you can. It's about your father." His voice sounded somber, and my heart started pounding. What could my father's lawyer have to tell me? I pressed SAVE and then called him back right away. The call went to voice mail and I hung up. Then I decided to call Rosie, but the call went to voice mail as well. I took a deep breath and looked at the Manhattan skyline as we drove across the bridge.

My mind was running a hundred miles a minute as I realized that something still felt off. Very, very off. I didn't know what was going on, but for some reason I knew this wasn't the end. I made up my mind in that moment that I wasn't going to stop my search for the truth. There were still too many unknowns, and I was going to find out exactly what was going on. I was surprised at my fervor, after everything that had happened. Maybe it was that Jakob had just let me leave, or his comments about my parents' marriage. Maybe it was that Rosie had only called once. Maybe it was that Larry had called to talk about my father. Maybe it was everything combined. Whatever it was. I knew this wasn't the end. I wasn't done. I still didn't have the truth. Yes, my heart was broken. Yes, I felt scared and unsafe. Yes, I didn't know whom I trusted or if I could even trust my own thoughts and emotions, but I knew that I wasn't giving up. Not now. I wasn't about to disappear as Jakob had suggested. I was going to get to the bottom of this.

Jakob must have had a reason to kidnap me. Aside from just trying to scare me and figure out what I knew. That couldn't have been it. My heart felt hollow as I thought about Jakob. My stomach sank as I thought about his clear blue eyes and his light kisses. I closed my eyes and thought back to my time on the island. I could almost smell the salt water and I could feel the slight sting in my eyes after swimming all day. I could remember the feel of the wind on my face as my hair hit my cheek. If I concentrated hard enough, I could feel Jakob's lips on my skin, his fingers grabbing my waist and pulling me toward him. I could feel the heat in my stomach as his erection pushed into me. I could feel his need, his desire, his passion. My throat caught as I opened my eyes. It had all been a lie. An illusion. Jakob had never cared about me.

"I can't get up into the middle. You have to walk. That okay?"

"That's fine." I pulled out my cash. "How much?"

"Fifty dollars."

"Here you go." I handed him three $20 bills. "Keep the change."

"Thanks." He grinned. "Need help with anything?"

"No." I shook my head, grabbed my bag, and got out of the car. I slammed the door and disappeared into the crowd without another word. It felt weird to be back in the sea of tourists and natives all walking somewhere with a purpose. All going their own ways, not bothering to pay attention to those around them. What stories did these people have? Where were they from? What did they do for a living? What secrets did they hold? Why were they really here? I felt safe in the crowd of nameless and faceless people. I knew why I was here. I was here to remember what it felt like to be in a city with millions of people. Something in the sounds of beeping horns, screaming kids, and buskers was beautiful. The cacophony allowed my mind to focus on something other than the deception that had occupied my every second for the last two days.

I walked down the pedestrian mall in the center of Times Square and stared up at the bright lights surrounding me. They advertised Broadway shows, businesses, TV shows, everything and nothing. I spun around until I felt dizzy. Stopping, I looked around to see if anyone was watching, but no one was paying attention to me. It made me smile, and then I started laughing. I could do anything I wanted and no one would think it was strange—I would just be part of the makeup of the city. That was why I loved New York—anything and everything was accepted. Though that was part of the reason I hated it as well. I didn't want to be nameless. I wanted to be noticed. I wanted . . .

My phone beeped and I grabbed it from my bag. I frowned at the text message from "unknown." *It's not over yet, Bianca. It's not over until everyone pays. Enjoy the bright lights. Darkness will soon be yours again, but don't fear. I'm always here.*

I dropped the phone and looked around me slowly. Was Jakob here? Who had sent the text? Was I being watched? I shivered as I bent down to pick up the phone, relieved to see that it hadn't broken.

*Who is this?* I texted back, but a failure message bounced back to me right away: *Sorry, this phone doesn't accept text messages.*

Frowning, I put the phone back in my bag. I walked over to the McDonald's and took a seat against a wall. All of a sudden, the random crowds of people didn't seem so safe anymore.

Pulling out my phone again, I called the only other person I could think of. The one person I knew had to know something.

"Bianca," David answered on the second ring, and I almost cried out in relief.

"David, is that you?"

"Yes." He sighed and lowered his voice. "What are you doing?"

"I'm back in New York."

"What?" His voice dropped even lower and I could hear the shock in his voice.

"Surprised Mattias let me go?"

"Bianca, you're not safe." He sounded worried. "I don't understand what's going on."

"What are you talking about? Why didn't you tell me about Mattias? He kidnapped me, David. I was on a—"

"Bianca, listen to me. You need—"

"How could you do this to me? Why didn't you tell me?" I was so emotional, I couldn't even think straight. "I really liked you, David, and you used me. You should have—"

"Bianca, I wasn't using you." He sighed. "Listen to me, please. Let me help you."

"Why? Why should I trust you?" I cried out. I could see several people staring at me as I talked. I jumped up and walked out of the McDonald's and down the street quickly. The lack of safety in the crowd could not outweigh my need to hold a private conversation.

"Bianca, there are things you don't know."

"Yeah, I gathered that."

"Where are you?" he whispered. "Let me—"

"Hold on," I whispered into the phone as I stopped at a

newsstand and stared at the front page of that day's *Times.* The headline read, "FTC Approves $10 billion Bradley Inc. Merger, Deal Signed This Week."

"I gotta go." I hung up fast before quickly picking up the newspaper to read the article.

"Hey, lady, this isn't the library. You buying that paper?"

"How much?"

"What does it say on the paper?" he snapped.

I handed him a twenty. "Keep the change." I walked away quickly and heard him muttering something about entitled trust-fund kids. As if. I walked to the corner, stepped back against the wall, and opened the paper so I could read the article about Bradley Inc. I read it ferociously, swallowing every detail whole and letting it fill my mind. As I read it a second time to make sure I'd fully understood, my jaw dropped.

Bradley Inc. was being purchased by another corporation and last week had been the week when the information went public. The paperwork was to be signed in the upcoming days and then the merger would be complete. I didn't understand all the intricacies of the article, but everything in me was telling me that this was why I'd been taken to that island. Mattias wanted to make sure that I wasn't around to ruin the merger. However, why had he let me come back before the merger was complete? It didn't make any sense. Unless he knew that it was too late for me to stop the merger. Or if he cared about me more than he cared about the merger. I wanted to slap myself for my last thought. *Wishful thinking, Bianca.*

I pulled out my phone again and tried to call Larry.

Unfortunately the call went to voice mail again. I'd call him again tomorrow, but for now I needed to go home. I needed a good night's sleep, and I needed to digest everything that had happened the last couple of weeks.

I decided to walk back to my apartment instead of taking a cab. I still hadn't counted how much cash I'd been given, and I didn't want to spend it all before I had a chance to figure out whether I still had a job, or what else had changed in my absence. I had just reached my door when my phone rang.

I answered quickly, expecting to hear Larry's voice. "Hello?"

"Bianca." It was Jakob, his tone soft and silky. I was immediately transported back to the island and his arms.

"What are you doing?"

"How are you?"

"I'm sure you already know. You've been following me."

"What?" His tone changed.

"I got the text message saying it wasn't over."

"What text message?"

"Don't play dumb." I opened the bag and was glad to see my keys in there.

"Bianca, what did the text message say?"

"Why should I tell you what you already know?" I looked behind me as I opened the door to my building and hurried in, running up the stairs as quickly as I could. I heard him sighing as I ran, but I didn't say anything.

"I trust you found your apartment as you left it?"

“Why are you calling me?” I snapped.

“Bianca, listen to me. I’m not the bad guy here.”

“You didn’t kidnap me?”

“I did.” His voice was hoarse.

“And you didn’t know I am Bianca London, daughter of—”

“I knew who you are,” he cut me off. “Listen to me, Bianca, there are things that you don’t know.”

“I know that. Neither you or David have to tell me that again.”

“You spoke to David?” His voice was short and I could tell from his tone that that upset him. Why would he care if I spoke to David?

“Yes.”

“Listen to me, Bianca. David cannot be trusted.”

“Uh-huh.”

“He’s not your friend.”

“And you are?”

“Bianca, do you remember on the island I told you I would never let anything happen to you? You have to trust me.”

“You made a mistake letting me go. The merger’s not complete.”

“The merger’s not complete?” He repeated my words softly. “What?”

“The paperwork hasn’t been signed yet. I can still make sure it doesn’t go through.”

"The merger with Bradley Inc.?" He spoke slowly, his voice furious. "You know about that?"

"Yup, you made a mistake. It hasn't been finalized. I read the newspaper today."

"Fuck! It shouldn't have been in the paper. It was meant to be private until it all went through. He lied."

"Who lied?"

"Bianca, listen to me. Do *not* trust David. Please do not do anything. I'm coming back. I'm coming to see you. You're not safe."

"That's what David said as well." I opened the door to my apartment and walked in slowly, my head thudding.

"Bianca, listen to me."

"No," I said weakly. "I don't trust you."

"Bianca, I miss you. You have to trust me. I let you go as you asked. I made a—"

"Good-bye, Mattias." I hung up quickly and closed the door behind me and leaned back. My eyes felt heavy with unshed tears and I took a deep breath. Why had Jakob called me? And if he hadn't texted me, who had? I walked into my apartment and looked around. Everything looked just as I'd left it. I sank down into the couch and held a cushion to me. What was I going to do?

I had no idea. Tears fell from my eyes and dropped onto the cushion as I sat there. Then I remembered the envelope in my bag. I ripped it open and pulled out a letter—it was from Jakob. I stared at it for a few seconds and then sat back before reading it.

*What we had was beautiful. I'm sorry I broke your trust. We were both there for a reason. I never went to take advantage of you. The feelings I had for you were real. The reasons I took you there were valid. You're right to be afraid. I don't control everything. You do not know everything. I will fight for the truth. My whole life has been building up to this moment. I cannot let you change that.*

*Jakob.*

I dropped the letter on my couch and stood up in disgust. His letter meant nothing to me. *He* meant nothing to me. I didn't want to remember the way he'd gone out of his way to find coconuts for me, so I could drink the water and eat the pulp. Or the hours he'd spent in the ocean trying to catch fish. Or the nights I'd spent in his arms, cuddled up next to his chest as he'd run his fingers across my hair and back, kissing me softly as his eyes told me all the other things he wanted to do to me.

He'd been playing me from the start. He'd taken me to that island with the sole purpose of making me fall for him. And he wanted to make sure that I didn't see any money from Bradley Inc. Jakob didn't care about me. He never had and I needed to remember that. I needed to sleep. I needed to forget him. I needed to bring him and his family down. I knew that I had to be stronger, better, wiser, more fearless. The Bradley family had fooled my parents and now me. I wasn't going to let them get away with it again. I crawled into bed and fell into a deep sleep within seconds of my head hitting the pillow.

I awoke the next morning feeling tense and uneasy, despite the sound of birds chirping outside my window. I climbed out of bed and walked into the living room, feeling disoriented. I frowned as I saw the letter on the coffee table. I could have sworn that I'd left it on the couch. My heart started thudding as I heard a loud creak behind me. I turned around quickly, but nobody was there.

Taking a deep breath, I read the letter again. All color fell from my face as I saw a note scrawled on the bottom of the paper: *This is not over, Bianca. Mattias.* I was positive I had not seen that part of the note the night before. That meant someone had been in my apartment when I was sleeping. I hurried to the door—it was still locked, and it didn't look as if anyone had broken in. I heard another creak and turned around slowly, my fingers shaking as I heard a buzzing in my ears. Was someone in the apartment with me? I stood next to the door, frozen in fear. Then my phone rang. I ran over to the couch and picked the phone up, my heart racing.

"Hello?"

"Bianca?" It was Rosie. "Where have you been? Who is the guy you left the bar with? Why haven't you called me?"

"Rosie?" I sank onto the couch. "Oh, Rosie." My voice trembled.

"Oh my God, Bianca, what's wrong?" She sounded worried. "Did he rape you?"

"Did who rape me?" I asked in confusion.

"The guy you left the bar with."

"Rosie, I didn't leave the bar with anyone. I was kidnapped."

"What?" she screamed. "What?"

"Rosie"—I started crying—"I'm scared. I think someone is after me."

"What's going on, Bianca?"

"I think someone might be in the apartment with me right now," I whispered into the phone, my body frozen on the couch. I was still listening to Rosie's voice over the phone, but all my other senses were on high alert to what was going on in my apartment.

"What are you talking about?"

"I think someone broke into my apartment." I took a deep breath and stood up. "I'm going to check."

"Are you crazy?" Rosie sounded shocked. "Leave the apartment now and call the police."

"Stay on the phone with me," I said softly as I walked to the kitchen quickly. I grabbed a knife from my butcher block and took a deep breath. "I'm going to check now."

"Bianca, this doesn't sound like a good idea." Rosie spoke quickly. "Please just leave your apartment and call the police!"

"It's fine." As I crept past the couch, I heard the loud creak in front of me again and nearly jumped out of my skin. My face was burning and my stomach was a bundle of nerves, but then I stepped back and forward again and I heard the same creak. "It's the floorboards." I breathed a sigh of relief. "It's just the floorboards. Stupid old apartment."

"Are you sure?"

"Let me check." I walked into my bedroom and looked inside the closets quickly, the knife held in front of me as I surveyed all the small spaces. "I'm going into the bathroom now." I pushed the door open and jumped back before moving forward and checking. "It's all clear."

"You're scaring me, Bianca. What's going on?"

"Can you come over so we can talk in person?" I asked softly. "Please."

"I'll come over now," she said passionately. "Oh my God, what happened to you, Bianca?"

"Just come over," I sobbed, my composure breaking again now that I knew I was alone.

"I'm on my way."

She hung up and I sat back and closed my eyes, letting the tears flow freely.

Then my phone beeped again—a new text. *Be careful, Bianca. You can't trust anyone.*

The text was from the number Jakob had called me from the night before. I deleted the text and closed my eyes. Why was he tormenting me? What more did he want from me? Then another text came through. I grabbed my phone angrily, ready to give Jakob a piece of my mind, but this time it wasn't from him.

*You looked so peaceful last night as you tossed and turned in bed. Maybe next time I'll stay and keep you warm.*

I stared at the text message and frowned. Why was Jakob sending me text messages from two different numbers? Why was he calling me and threatening me at the same time? It didn't make any sense. Unless Jakob hadn't been lying when he said he hadn't sent that text. My body felt cold as I remembered something he'd said about Steve—Jakob had been confused about Steve's going crazy as well. That hadn't been a part of his plan. And if that hadn't been a part of his plan, then someone else had a role in everything. And I needed to find out who that was.

Maybe Mattias wasn't the mastermind after all. Maybe it was David. After all, what did I really know about him?

# four

"Bianca!" I could hear Rosie banging on the door. "Open up."

I walked to the door and opened it slowly, staring at her for a few seconds before she pulled me into her arms.

"Oh, Bianca," she said in a soft tone.

"Why didn't you just let yourself in?" I mumbled against her shoulder, happy to finally be with someone I trusted.

"I let myself into the building but didn't want to just come into the apartment in case I scared you. Oh my God, Bianca, what happened to you?"

"I don't even know where to start." I sighed and closed the door. "Let's sit down."

"What were you talking about when you said someone kidnapped you? What's going on, Bianca?" Rosie's voice was frantic as she gazed at me. "You're freaking me out."

"I don't really know what's going on." I bit my lower lip. "Do you still have my handbag from the night in the bar?"

"Yeah, I brought it with me. I thought it was weird you left it." She looked thoughtful. "I'm so sorry, I don't know why I just believed the bartender. I didn't think you would do something like that, but I figured maybe you had a few drinks and got carried away and you know . . ."

"You thought I just needed to get laid?"

"Yeah." She closed her eyes. "I know that's not you, though. I know you wouldn't hook up with a guy you just met. Well, not unless he's absolutely gorgeous."

"Do you remember I told you I thought the Bradleys had something to do with my mother's death?"

"Yeah." She frowned. "Why?"

"Mattias Bradley kidnapped me."

"No way!" Her eyes widened in shock.

"Did you bring your Balenciaga bag with you?" Yes, it was still slung over her shoulder. "Did you take out my papers?"

"What papers?" She frowned as I pulled the bag off her arm and opened it eagerly, my heart racing. I dug my way through her makeup and let out a sigh of relief as my fingers felt the slickness of the plastic bag. She hadn't taken it out. I pulled out the bag and rifled through the copied documents I'd hidden, feeling as if I'd just won the lottery. "You still have them."

"What are they?" She sat down next to me and frowned as I held the pages next to my heart.

"Documents that prove that the Bradleys were involved in my mother's death and that I'm a rightful owner of Bradley Inc."

"No way!" Her jaw dropped. "Really?" She looked annoyed at herself. "I really need to start cleaning out my purse more regularly."

"Well, I don't know exactly. . . . I mean, I need to speak to my father's attorney to see what legal rights I have, but I'm pretty sure these documents make pretty damning evidence."

"Wow. And I had them all this time and didn't even know." She shook her head and gazed at me in shock. "These are the originals?"

"Oh, no." I bit my lower lip. "The originals are in a safe place, my security-deposit box. But I'm not going there to retrieve them now; someone is still trying to scare me off."

"You're scaring me, Bianca." Rosie's face was white. "Why were you kidnapped and how? And what do you mean someone is trying to scare you off?"

"When we were at the bar, someone drugged me or something. I woke up after I passed out in the back of a car with a man. And then we were taken to a deserted island and left there. I thought he'd been kidnapped as well, but he hadn't—he was the one who planned it. Rosie, Mattias Bradley kidnapped me! I read in the newspapers yesterday that Bradley Inc. is merging with some other company, and I think I was kidnapped so I couldn't stop the merger from going through. I think they were scared I'd stake my claim on the company, and as a major shareholder, they couldn't do anything without me."

"Are you saying you're rich?" Rosie's eyes lit up.

"What?" I frowned, too caught up in my own story to follow her train of thought.

"If you're a part owner of Bradley Inc., that would mean you're rich rich rich!" she gushed.

I gave her a weak smile. Was that really her response to everything I'd just said? Then I remembered something she'd told me before I'd been kidnapped. "Didn't you tell me you were working on some deal for Bradley, or trying to land some big deal?"

"Yeah, we were." She nodded. "We had a few meetings, but we didn't get the contract."

"Did you meet Mattias Bradley, then?" I stared at her face thoughtfully.

"No." She shook her head and stared right into my eyes. "I wish I had, though. I would have slapped him hard for you." She grabbed my hands and squeezed them. "So what are you going to do now? Call the police?"

"I don't think I can call the police." I shook my head. "My story sounds fantastical. What would I even say? No, I need to think of something else." I closed my eyes for a few seconds and tried to ignore the image of Jakob's face in my mind. "Something doesn't seem right."

"What do you mean?"

"I don't know." I opened my eyes slowly and bit my lower lip. "Everything doesn't add up."

"What was Mattias like? Did he hurt you?"

"No, he didn't hurt me." A dagger of pain ran through

me. "I don't know what to say about him. I don't know how to feel. He was nice—different, but nice. And he was handsome—oh, boy, was he handsome. He had piercing blue eyes that seemed to see into my soul. His arms were sinewy and strong, and his chest was hard as rock, but so soft to the touch." My voice trailed off as Rosie's eyes narrowed.

"What do you mean, 'soft to the touch'?"

"Nothing." My face turned bright red.

"Bianca London!" she screeched. "You hooked up with him?"

"I . . ."

"You hooked up with the man who kidnapped you?"

"I didn't know then that he was the one who kidnapped me." I bit my lower lip. "I thought he was an innocent bystander like me." Rosie was already looking confused, so I told her everything from the beginning—from waking up with Jakob on the beach, to Steve's arrival, all the way to our rescue and the phone call I'd heard in Jakob's hotel room.

I shook my head angrily. "I should have known better. I should have known it didn't make sense."

"So . . . was Jakob good?"

"Rosie!" I exclaimed loudly as I blushed. "He was the best."

"Oh."

"I know." I shrugged. "Isn't that life?"

"I can't believe he slept with you, knowing he'd kidnapped you."

"Do you think he cared?" I shook my head. "He had me fooled, especially when Steve came."

"Did Steve try and harm you then?" Rosie asked softly. "You must have felt so betrayed to learn that Mattias knew Steve before he came to the island."

"I was. I couldn't believe that he could have lied to me so thoroughly. I couldn't believe that he could have held me in his arms and made me think that . . ." My voice caught and I took a deep breath. "I've never felt so disillusioned in my whole life, Rosie. I've never trusted someone so much, only to have them turn on me like that."

"Did you really trust him, though?" she asked skeptically. "I mean, you didn't really know him."

"When I gave myself to him, it was with complete trust. Yes, I had some fears, yes, I wasn't sure who he was, but deep inside I was positive he was a good guy. I was positive he would never hurt me."

"Men lie all the time," she sneered. "They say they love you, that they want to take care of you, but it's funny how quickly they forget about you."

"Or it's just one big lie." I nodded. "My heart is broken. I feel like Liesl in *The Sound of Music* when she realizes her beau is a Nazi."

"Huh?" Rosie frowned. "Who?"

"What was his name again? Was it Friedrich?" I thought carefully. "No, Friedrich was her brother. You know who I mean, they sang the 'I am sixteen' song."

"Bianca, I have no idea what you're talking about."

"Do you remember when Maria and the von Trapp family perform that song, toward the end of the movie, and they're hiding out? And Liesl's boyfriend or crush or whatever finds them and she says, 'Please don't say anything,' but he betrays her and calls the rest of the Nazis over to take them in. Rolf! That was it, his name was Rolf."

"Okay." Rosie stared at me as if wondering if I'd lost it.

"My point being"—I sighed—"that I was betrayed and you can't trust anyone. Not even someone you think has your back. Not even someone you think you love." I jumped up then, not wanting to talk about it anymore.

"You should call your dad's attorney," Rosie said softly. "If he gave you all of these papers, then maybe he knows more than he's letting on."

"Yeah, perhaps." I nodded. I was about to tell her that someone had added a line to the letter Jakob had given me while I'd been sleeping, but I didn't want her to know about the letter. I didn't want her to think that Mattias was still threatening me. I didn't want her to tell me that I had to come and stay with her. I knew that would be the smartest thing to do, but I wasn't going to let someone drive me out of my home. "Yeah, let me call him." I grabbed my phone from the table and made a call.

"Hello," a teary-sounding voice answered.

"Is Larry there, please?"

"Who is this?" She sounded panicked.

"It's Bianca London."

"Bianca?" The voice froze. "Bianca London, did you say?"

"Yes, I need to speak to Larry, please, it's urgent."

"Larry's gone missing." Her voice dropped. "This is his wife."

"What do you mean, he's gone missing?" My heart stopped and my body grew cold at her words. How could he have gone missing? He was the only one who could help me. And then I realized that of course he'd gone missing. Mattias didn't want me to find out the truth. First Steve was missing and now Larry? How convenient that both the men who could give me answers had disappeared.

"I was out shopping." She gasped. "I just went to get some new clothes. We were going to go on a cruise. Larry wanted us to take a vacation. But while I was out, he called me, said that he thinks someone is in the house. He said that his old friend's daughter is in trouble. That he shouldn't have kept quiet."

"What old friend?" I whispered frantically. I could feel Rosie's eyes staring at my back.

"I can't remember, but he said he owed his daughter, Bianca, the truth. I remember the name because it's Mick Jagger's ex wife's name and I love the Rolling Stones."

"What truth does he owe me?"

"I don't know." She started crying. "The phone disconnected, and when I got home, the house was ransacked and he was gone. All the papers in his office were on the floor, and I think there were drops of blood as well."

"Did you call the police?"

"Yes." She sounded frantic. "But they have no leads. He was taken, Bianca. I'm positive he was taken."

"I'm so sorry. I don't know what to say." My head was spinning. "Did he say anything else?"

"He told me that I should call you, Bianca. I didn't call yet because I was too upset. But he told me to tell you to look through the papers carefully. He said, 'The answers are in the papers, but the truth might not be.' "

"The papers he gave me in the box?" I questioned frantically. "And what answers? Is he talking about my mother's death? Is he talking about my dad still being an owner in Bradley Inc.?"

"I don't know," she sobbed. "I have to go. All I can tell you is what he said, 'The answers are in the papers, but the truth might not be.' "

" 'But not the truth'? Did he say 'but the truth might not be' or did he say 'but not the truth'?" My mind was swirling a hundred miles a minute. What did that mean? And which statement had he actually spoken? If he'd said "but the truth might not be," then the information in the papers might be valid. However, if he'd said "but not the truth," it seemed to me that all of the answers I'd come up with might be false. "The answers are in the papers" indicated that clues were in the papers he'd given me, but maybe the clues weren't as straightforward as I'd thought them to be.

"I don't remember. I have to go. I'm sorry." She hung up.

I held the phone to my ear for a few seconds, hoping that she hadn't really hung up. I needed to know more.

What did Larry's comment mean? What did he know? And more important, where was he? Had Jakob kidnapped him as well?

"What's going on, Bianca?" Rosie touched my shoulder, and I turned around slowly. I looked at her, but my eyes couldn't focus on her face. I wanted to be alone. I needed to go through the papers again. I had to have missed something. *The answers are in the papers, but not the truth.*

All of a sudden I wasn't so sure of the conclusions I'd made by reading all the papers my father had left for me. Things weren't adding up, not the way they should be. I needed to analyze the information the papers held. My brain was throbbing with a dull excitement. There were answers to be found, and I was going to find them. I had to do this for both my mother and my father. There were too many questions and I wasn't going to sit passively by and wait for the truth to hit me on the head. I was going to figure this puzzle out.

Why had Jakob let me go before the merger had been finalized? Why had Steve turned rogue? Where was Steve? And where was Larry? What did Larry's message mean? Who had been in my apartment the night before? Was Jakob the one sending me the threatening texts as well? Had Mr. Bradley had my mother killed because he wanted to gain control of the company? All of a sudden, everything that had seemed so simple seemed weak and hazy. I'd thought this was just about proving that Jeremiah Bradley had stolen my father's shares and had my mother killed. I'd been naive enough to think I could just get the information I needed and move on. I'd gone into this whole thing thinking it would be easy gaining access to the company through David. Whom had I been kidding? I was swimming with sharks, sharks that ate fish like me for breakfast.

"Bianca?"

I blinked at Rosie, feeling cold inside. My arms had goose bumps and a hollowness was in my soul. My brain rattled as the unanswered questions knocked against my skull.

"Sorry. He wasn't in," I said quickly, and walked back to the couch.

"Oh, that's it?" Rosie looked surprised. "You seemed to be having a longer conversation than just that."

"She said that he had a message for me, but she couldn't remember it." I sank onto the couch and offered Rosie a weak smile. I wasn't sure why I was lying to her. Something about the whole situation made me feel too uneasy. Too many holes were appearing in what I thought I knew. I wanted to stew on it all first. I felt guilty as I stared at her furrowed brows. I could tell that she didn't believe me. "I'm feeling slightly tired." I yawned and stretched. "I think I need a good night's sleep."

"It's still morning." She stared at me unblinking.

"Well, a midmorning siesta, like they do in Spain." I paused. "Well, maybe not technically a siesta, but you know what I mean."

"But you're not Spanish."

"I just need a rest. I've had a long week, Rosie. What with

being kidnapped and all." I offered her a weak smile, but she stared at me with no answering look of understanding.

"Bianca, you've just been kidnapped. You've had sex with the man that kidnapped you. You lost your dad recently. You've been through a lot. I really don't want to leave you alone."

"I'll be fine."

"How can you be sure that Mattias won't kidnap you again?"

"Well, he let me go. . . ." I shrugged.

"Why, though? Why would he do that?"

"I don't know." A sick feeling hit my stomach and I felt the danger of my situation spreading through me. He had to have let me go for a reason. It didn't make sense. *Unless he fell for you*, a small voice in my head whispered to me. I frowned at the little devil in my head. She was getting my hopes up and that was the last thing that I needed.

"It just doesn't sound plausible, Bianca. Why would someone do that?"

"Sherlock Holmes said that it only has to be possible, not probable," I muttered obstinately. "If something is possible, it can still be true." *He could like me for real, he really could.*

"You're confusing me." She plopped down next to me. "What's going on, Bianca? What else happened to you? Where were you?" She touched my shoulder. "Let me help you."

"I don't want to talk about it right now. I'm sorry. I'm just so tired. Thank you for coming over. Come back for dinner?" I gave her an apologetic smile and yawned. "I just really need to sleep for a few hours. My brain has been in overdrive and I'm physically and mentally exhausted."

"I have a date tonight," she said hesitantly. "But I can come—"

"No, you don't need to come back tonight." I offered her a smile, not wanting her to see how relieved I felt. "I feel awful. I still don't know much about your boyfriend or anything. I'm sorry."

"It's fine." She clasped my hand. "We can talk about it later." She sighed as she stared at me. "I don't know if I want you to be alone. What if someone comes back and tries to kidnap you again? What are you going to do now? I don't want to just leave you."

"I'm going to sleep and then I'm going to see if I can watch some movies and write some articles and get my mind off of this whole ordeal for a few hours." Not that that would be possible. There was no way that I'd be able to just watch a movie, but I didn't want Rosie to know that. I jumped up off the couch and Rosie stood up as well. I ran my hands through my hair and stifled a half yawn.

"I guess you do need sleep." She stepped back. "I don't want to just leave you by yourself, I just got here."

"I'll be okay. It was good to see you. I just need to rest, then I'll be able to tell you everything. I just don't want to go through all of it right now." I smiled an apology. "I'm sorry."

"Don't be sorry, Bianca." She reached over and hugged

me. "I'm the one who should be sorry. I'm the one who blew it. I'm going to make it up to you, I promise."

"It's okay. I'm just glad to have you as a friend." I squeezed her hand. "I'm not sure what I'd do if I didn't have you in my life. You're my best friend and I know I can always count on you."

"Call me if you need anything." She walked toward the door and then looked back at me. "And if you need to talk or figure anything out, I'm here."

"Thanks, Rosie." I got up and walked her to the door, then locked it behind her. I felt lighter once she was out of the apartment and I wasn't sure why. I hurried back to my couch so I could look through the papers again, to see if there were any clues that I'd missed. I opened the plastic bag that I'd removed from Rosie's purse and pulled out a stack of papers, still feeling unsettled about my conversation. Something she'd said had put me on edge, but I wasn't sure what it was. I couldn't put my finger on it, but something felt off.

"Get it together, Bianca." I shook my head and tried to gather my thoughts. I wasn't sure if I was imagining things now. Maybe I was just feeling discombobulated due to everything that had gone on. My head was throbbing and my whole body was on edge as I sat there. It was as if I were still waiting for something to happen. I couldn't relax and I had no idea what I was going to do next.

~

"The answers are in the papers, but not the truth," I mumbled as I stared at the patent and corporation forms in my hands. "What answers?" I frowned as I stared at the words. Everything had seemed so clear when I'd first gotten the papers. My dad had been a partner. He'd been the inventor. He thought my mom had been murdered and the Bradleys had something to do with it. What, then, was wrong with this picture? What was I missing—and where had Larry gone?

The loud beeping of cars outside reminded me that I'd been tied up in the back of a car not long ago. And I still didn't know why. I wanted to talk to Jakob. I wanted to—I stopped in midthought as I stared at the corporation papers one more time. The law firm that had drawn up the contract was Larry's. Larry, my father's attorney, had been involved with Bradley, London, and Maxwell. He'd had access to all the legal information. It struck me that he had to know a lot more than he'd let on. My heart racing, I reread the incorporation papers once again, and realized that the next best person I could talk to would be Maxwell, or someone related to Maxwell. I hadn't had any luck finding any information on Maxwell, but I hadn't spent much time trying to find him. I'd put all my energy into the Bradleys, and now it was time for me to expand my search.

I grabbed my phone before I could change my mind and called David.

"Bianca?" he asked, sounding surprised. "How are you?"

"I need to see you." I didn't hesitate. I couldn't afford to be unsure or to hesitate. I needed to forge ahead with my investigation and ignore the fleeting panic that had settled in my stomach.

"When?"

"Are you free for dinner tonight?" I held my breath as I waited for his answer.

"You want to go to dinner?" His tone changed to one of expectation. A small smile broke out on my face. David was still interested in me. I could use that to my advantage. I wasn't stupid enough to think that he liked me more than anything except as a potential conquest. I knew enough about men to know that they liked a challenge.

I softened my voice. "If you're free, I'd like to chat." I couldn't afford to be too obvious.

"I don't know." He sounded unsure.

"You owe me, David. I trusted you. I want some answers."

"I swear I didn't know what Mattias had planned," he said quickly, and I tried not to roll my eyes. *Sure, you didn't.* I gripped the phone tightly. As long as he thought I wanted to know about Mattias, he might have his guard down about other subjects; especially if I brought them up casually.

"I've missed you. I was thinking about you on the island," I lied. "I was wishing things could have been different between us."

"Yeah. You never got to experience a night with me and we never got to—" His voice was husky and I felt my stomach churning. I had no romantic inklings toward David anymore, not even to kissing. I knew I'd have to pretend I was still attracted to him, even if he now revolted me. I'd make him feel that he was obliged to be my Prince Charming. If he wasn't a sociopath, it would work—but I knew that was also a gamble.

"So, tonight?" I cut him off, not wanting to go down the innuendo road. The last thing I needed was for him to show up thinking that tonight was going to be the night we were going to seal the deal.

"Meet me at a cute place called the Little Owl. It's in the West Village, on Grove Street."

"Okay. What time?"

"Seven?"

"That's fine." I nodded gratefully. "Thanks for this, David."

"You've nothing to thank me for, yet."

He hung up and I sat back on the couch, my breathing labored. Part of me was scared that David was going to ambush me. What if he arrived with someone else? What if I was kidnapped again? It scared me to be making such a big move without thinking it through properly. Though this time, I wouldn't be a sitting duck. I jumped up and went to the kitchen, fishing a serrated knife out of the cutlery drawer. I wanted to take my butcher's knife, but it wouldn't fit into my handbag. I wrapped the one I had chosen in a paper towel and placed it in my handbag. At times like this I wished I owned a gun, a small pistol or something.

I stared at the wall clock in front of me and sighed deeply. I had a few hours left to do research before I had to start getting ready for my meeting with David. I was going to have to scrub up and shave every part of my body before I left the house. I wanted to show up looking like a femme fatale. I wanted him to take one look at me and think to himself, *I will do anything to have this woman, I will tell her whatever she wants to know.* I knew that women had a certain power over certain men. I knew that there was power in sex, or the promise of sex. David was my best bet—and my only bet right now—to find out exactly what had happened all those years ago.

~

The Little Owl was a cozy restaurant on the corner of two quiet streets. The red facade and blue awnings made me smile. This place didn't take itself too seriously. I walked inside and smiled at the commonplace wooden tables and chairs. This wasn't fancy or ostentatious. I immediately felt comfortable.

"Bianca!" David stood up and waved to me from a table by the wall, his face bright as he watched me walking toward him. I stopped at the table and took in his appearance. It was hard not to compare him to Jakob. Next to Jakob, David was a boy. Handsome, yes, but roguishly attractive, no. His face and build seemed almost babyish when compared to Jakob's wall of muscle and sinew. David was a prince to Jakob's king.

"Hello, David." I smiled at him weakly as he stepped forward to give me a kiss. I turned my cheek quickly so his lips didn't meet mine. I saw a slight frown on his face and knew it was going to be harder than I'd thought to fake it with him.

"You look stunning." His eyes showed their appreciation for the efforts I'd made.

"Thank you." I nodded and took a seat as he pulled my chair out. It was almost as if we were on a first date and his brother hadn't kidnapped me.

"How are you?" He took a seat across from me and I kept my face passive, though a storm was brewing inside me. *How do you think I am, motherfucker?* I smiled weakly and turned to the side. My body froze as I saw someone on the street peering through the front window. I furrowed my brows to get another look. Was it Steve? My heart was racing and I looked back at David, searching his face to see if this was a setup.

"What's wrong?" He frowned and grabbed my hands.

*How could I ever have thought he was cute?* My stomach churned at the softness of his fingertips on my palms. "Nothing." I looked back toward the window and the figure was gone.

"You look great." He leaned forward. "Really beautiful."

"Better than what you expected for someone that just came back from being kidnapped?" I raised an eyebrow at him and pulled my hands back. I wasn't going to let him get away with this so easily.

"Bianca, I . . ." He sighed and sat back. "You're mad at me?"

"Are you joking?" I shook my head. "Am I mad at you?" I laughed bitterly. "What do you think?"

“Well, it sounds as though you have some anger toward me.” He pursed his lips, and I think only then did he understand that this wasn’t about to be a night of hot sex between the two of us.

I leaned forward and went on the offensive. “Why did Mattias kidnap me?” This was my new strategy. I was going to go hard on the Mattias angle, even though I knew David was unlikely to tell me the truth. I hoped if I pushed hard on that point, he would answer my other questions without becoming suspicious.

“You were asking too many questions.” He shrugged.

“Did he kidnap me because he was worried I’d stop the merger from going through?”

“Bianca”—he bit down on his lower lip—“I really don’t know what to tell you. Mattias makes these decisions without me. I wish I could tell you what he wanted.”

“Mattias told me something about Maxwell when we were on the island.” I causally sipped some water, hoping the redness in my face wasn’t betraying my lie.

“Oh yeah?” He picked up a bottle of wine and looked at my glass. “Would you like some?”

“No, thanks.” I shook my head. No way was I drinking wine with David. I didn’t want to be drugged, and I didn’t want to end up in his bed either. “I’m sticking to water.”

“Fair enough.” He placed the bottle back on the table. “Shall we order before we get back to the deep conversation?”

“If that’s what you want.”

"I recommend the arctic char, though the pork chop with brussels sprouts is divine as well."

"I'm not really a pork eater." I opened the menu and looked down. I couldn't afford to go too hard too fast or that would be it.

"You can't go wrong with any of their entrées."

"I might get the chicken." Safe, plain, boring chicken. It was pretty hard to mess chicken up and I'd know if it was raw.

"The chicken is good." He smiled widely. "So, Bianca, Bianca, Bianca, I was surprised when you called me."

"Why?"

"I don't know." He shrugged. "The fact that Mattias kidnapped you and tried to scare you on the island with his henchman Steve?" He looked at me with a sad expression. "I'm so sorry. If I'd had any idea what he was capable of, I never would have told him you were looking for him."

"So you knew?" I asked him softly, leaning forward. "When, exactly?"

"I—I—" He stuttered for a few seconds and looked at me with a sorrowful expression. "I thought he was joking when he told me his plan. I thought he was just saying stuff."

"Where is Steve?" My eyes never left David's face as I launched another question and waited to see his response.

"Steve?" He looked confused. "No idea, why?"

"Steve disappeared."

"What?" David frowned and looked away for a second. I could see a vein throbbing in his neck. "Mattias must have done something to him."

"He doesn't know where Steve is." I shook my head.

"That's not possible." David's voice was rough. "He has to know where Steve is. He's the one who sent Steve to the island. He thought it would be a good way to get you to trust him faster—said that the quickest way to make two people bond is to make them think they need to work together against a mutual enemy." David gulped some more wine. "Steve was working for him."

"Steve tried to kill him."

"What?" David's face paled. "No, that's not possible. That must have been part of the act."

"I don't think so." It occurred to me that neither David nor Jakob seemed to understand what had motivated Steve. "Are you lying to me, David?" My eyes narrowed and I could feel a new power surging through me. I *would* figure this out and get to the bottom of the situation.

"I swear to God. I don't know what Mattias is up to. I can't believe he would do all of this. You didn't deserve any of it, Bianca. I wish I could have protected you. I should have known better."

"How were you to know your brother was a sociopath?" I said, rolling my eyes.

"Exactly." David looked distraught. "I would have trusted him with my life. He's my blood." *Idiot.* I tried to hide my disdain for David from my face. How had he not realized I was being sarcastic?

"Do you know the attorney for Bradley Inc.?" I asked softly, then sipped some water.

"The attorney?" David frowned. "No, why?"

I bit my lower lip, considering, trying to decide whether to tell him about Larry's disappearance. I had to make a judgment call. Did I trust David? I knew the answer was no, but I also knew that I had to, a little bit. He was the soft brother. He looked devastated by what had happened. I knew he wasn't capable of the deception Jakob had pulled on me, especially not with our history.

"When my father died, my father's attorney gave me some papers. I just recently found out that my father's attorney was also the attorney for Bradley Inc., and, well, he's gone missing."

"Oh?" David sipped his wine and his eyes widened. "That doesn't seem like a coincidence, does it?"

*Bingo, Sherlock.* "No, it doesn't. I'm worried that something bad has happened to Larry."

"Do you know his last name?" David looked thoughtful.

"Renee." I stared at his face to see if his expression changed. "His name is Larry Renee."

"Never heard of him before." David shook his head, his expression blank.

"I think Mattias kidnapped him as well," I prodded on, hoping to see some sign of activity in David's brain. He couldn't be this clueless, could he?

"I wouldn't put it past him." David licked his lips. "Has he contacted you?"

"Who?"

"Mattias."

"No," I lied, though I wasn't sure why. "I don't know why he would contact me."

"He knows you know that he is Mattias, though?"

"Yes, he knows." I nodded. "He confirmed it."

"What happened on the island, Bianca?" David looked curiously at me. "What did my brother do to you?"

"What do you mean?"

"You've changed." His fingers circled the rim of his wine-glass. "You're more confident now."

"More confident?" I was surprised by his statement.

"Yes." He nodded. "Though, I suppose, you needed con-fidence to outwit Steve and Mattias."

"Who says I outwitted them?"

"You made it off the island." His face was solemn.

"You don't think that was their intention?"

"I know Mattias well." He half smiled. "In fact, I think I can say with certainty that I know him better than anyone else in the world. I don't think he intended for you to make it off the island. At least not right away."

"So why did he let me go?" *And why do you seem to think he had more nefarious reasons for taking me to the island if you thought he wasn't really going to kidnap me?*

"He knew he had to. If Steve had started doing crazy stuff, he knew it wasn't safe on the island anymore." David's eyes narrowed. "So he took you to one of his hotels in the Caribbean. He wanted to keep you there, but you found out the truth. Once you'd made him out to be Mattias, you called me, scared, and that's when you knew the truth. He didn't take you off the island to save you, Bianca. He most probably wanted to keep you in that hotel with him. He knew that you trusted him at that point, but then it blew up in his face. His lies came to surface and he had to let you go."

"Why did he have to let me go?"

"He must have known that I knew what was going on—he knew that I would save you. He knew that he couldn't keep you there against your will anymore."

"So he let me go because I called you?"

"I think you're safe because of me, yes." David nodded, a smug smile on his face.

"You think he wanted to harm me?" I said softly, not wanting to believe it.

"I don't know." David sipped some more wine. "I know Steve wasn't there with the best of intentions."

"Yeah." I frowned. Steve seemed to be the spanner in the works again. I was even more confused now. Whom was Steve working for? And why did David keep bringing Steve up? "What else do you know, David?"

Beep beep. My phone vibrated in my handbag and I reached in and grabbed it.

*I thought I told you not to see David*, the text read, and I frowned.

*Who is this?*

*Who do you think?*

*Jakob?*

*Leave the restaurant now.*

*Why?*

"Is everything okay?" David frowned at me and I looked up with a brief smile.

"Yeah, Rosie's texting me."

"Oh?" He cocked his head to the side. "I'm sure she's not happy to know you're dining with me."

"She always trusted you." I looked back down at the phone. "I'm sure she's not worried."

*Bianca, what are you hoping to get from dinner with my brother?*

*What I didn't get before.* I typed furiously, annoyed that Jakob thought he could tell me what to do. Then I paused. How did he know I was here?

*Don't you dare sleep with him.*

*I'll do what I want, Mattias.*

*You're playing into his hands.*

*Better his hands than yours.*

*You don't understand everything.*

*What don't I understand?* I waited for a few seconds and then messaged again. *How did you know I was at dinner with him?*

*There are many things I know.*

*Are you going to tell me what they are?*

*You don't understand the web you're in, Bianca.*

*I might not understand it, but I know you're the black widow.*

*It's easy to identify a black widow, and, yes, they can be more dangerous. However, the real danger lies with the brown recluse.*

*What does that mean?*

*Brown recluses are harder to identify and they leave a more permanent mark.*

*So which one are you?*

"Bianca"—David's green eyes were full of concern—"is everything okay? You're typing away."

"I'm fine. I'm just thinking." Why was Jakob warning me away from his brother, and why was David trying to convince me that Jakob wanted to harm me if they were both in this together?

"Thinking about what?"

"Nothing." I closed my bag and vowed to myself not to check my phone. I couldn't spend any more time texting Jakob when I had David right in front of me.

"You seem preoccupied."

"I'm fine. Well, as fine as I can be."

"You've had a major shock. I'm just sorry it was my brother who did this to you. I knew Mattias was slightly crazy, but I didn't think he would ever do anything like this."

"I don't really understand why I was kidnapped." I sipped some water. "I feel like I've been saying that a lot lately." I gave him a pointed look.

"Oh? To whom?"

"Well, Rosie and you and . . ." I sighed. "It doesn't matter."

"Whatever I can do to help you, Bianca, you just let me know."

"So are you excited about the merger?" I changed the subject as a waiter approached the table. He was young and cute and I didn't want to freak him out by letting him overhear a kidnapping conversation.

"You know I'm not really interested in that business stuff." David shrugged. "I get my check each month from the trust and that's good enough for me."

"Must be nice."

"Well, Mattias works hard so I don't have to." David made a face. "Sorry, I guess that was ill-timed."

"What I want to know is, who was signing the paperwork for this merger while Mattias and I were on the island?" Maybe that person was the reason why Steve had turned rogue.

"Maybe the COO or the attorneys?" David looked at me with a blank face and then turned to the waiter. "We'll have the soft-shell crab to start and the eggplant-Parm salad." David looked at me. "Did you see any other appetizers you wanted to try?"

"No, that's fine." I shook my head.

"Okay." He looked back at the waiter. "And a bottle of Bollinger."

"Yes, sir." The waiter grinned at the order of expensive champagne.

"I'm not drinking tonight, David."

"We must celebrate your safe return."

*It was a safe return, no thanks to you, no matter what you're trying to convince me of, David.* "I don't want to drink."

"One sip won't hurt you." His eyes danced as the waiter walked away. "I won't let you get into any trouble tonight."

"I don't think I got into any trouble the other night. Not

of my own doing." *I'm not going to sleep with you, if that's what you're hoping for.*

"The important thing is, you're safe now. There's no one that's going to get past me tonight."

*Let it all come out, David. Why don't you ask me to come stay the night in your bed, so you can protect me as well.* "Doesn't that make me feel safe?" I said sarcastically, studying his features dispassionately. Why had I been so mesmerized before with David? I'd gotten to the point where I'd even questioned my "investigation," but now I just found him annoying and condescending. And he wasn't helpful either. He'd never been helpful to me. He was just a lazy bum who lived off the family money. He would never tell me what I needed to know about Mattias or the company, not when that would endanger his own share of the income.

"So what are you going to do now?" He looked at me curiously. "Any plans for revenge?"

"I'm not trying to be funny, but do you think I would tell you that?" *Don't quit the day job to become a detective. Oh, wait, you don't have a day job.*

"Don't you trust me, Bianca?"

"Oh yeah, I trust you. I trust you like the Israelites trusted Moses."

"What?" He frowned. "What does that mean? They trusted him, right?"

"If you don't know, then you'll just have to read your Bible." I gave him a small smile to hide my annoyance. Did

I trust him? If he thought that, then he was dumber than he looked. However, I knew that I couldn't play him by being sarcastic and rude. I had to soften up with him.

"Do you ever think about us?" He leaned forward and grabbed my hands. The light of the candle made a shadow of his face on the wall behind him, and it struck me how calculated everything about him was. And also how dark and mysterious he was. What did I know about David? We'd dated for a few months, but everything had been predicated on my wanting to get closer to his brother. I didn't know David. And suddenly it struck me that that had been poor detective work on my part. In my haste to get to Mattias, I might inadvertently have missed out on access to more clues and information.

"Us?" I resisted the urge to pull my hands away and squeezed his fingers, letting them entwine with mine. This would make David think I still trusted him because he was obviously the cocky kind of sucker who believed his charm and good looks would win out in every situation. And this would also teach Jakob to spy on me. I looked around casually to see if anyone was paying attention. Who in the room was passing information on to Jakob?

"You know, you and me and when we dated." He grinned boyishly and his eyes darkened as he studied my face and the top of my chest. "I'm so sorry that I cheated on you. It wasn't because I didn't like you, but I had needs and, well, I wasn't strong enough to say no."

"It's fine, you did what you had to do." *And sticking your dick in another girl was what you thought you had to do. And I'm cool with that because I'm not sure I could look myself in the mirror knowing I slept with you.*

"It's you I think about, though," he whispered. "When I'm in bed with another girl, it's your face I see. It's you I want to be with. It's you I'm entering and making come. It's you calling out my name."

*That's not creepy at all, David.* "I see." I licked my lips nervously. Did he seriously think that would make me feel better? *Hey, Bianca, yeah, I cheated on you, but I was thinking about you every single time. Let's go back to my place now and make up for lost time.*

"I can still remember your taste." He sucked on his lower lip and stared at me. "So sweet and—"

*I'm going to throw up.* "We don't need to talk about this." My face reddened as I thought about the nights we'd spent together. A part of me felt icky knowing that I'd done physical things with both him and his brother. I didn't want to analyze it too closely. It wasn't as if I'd known they were related, and at least I hadn't had sex with David. That would have upped the creepy factor 10 percent at least.

"I guess I'm confused, then." He pulled his hands back and frowned. "Why are we here?"

"What do you mean, why are we here?" *Don't get annoyed, Bianca. You know he's not Sherlock or Watson or even Harriet the Spy's kid brother.*

"Why did you call me, Bianca? Why did you want to

meet?" He looked annoyed. "I thought it was because you'd realized you made a mistake."

*As if.* "That I'd made a mistake?" My jaw dropped. "You think I called you because I wanted to have sex with you?"

"Yes, no, not just that, obviously. I know you need support over what happened to you, but I don't have any answers for you, Bianca. I don't know why Mattias kidnapped you. I don't know why he let you loose. I don't know why he had Steve on the island with you. Maybe he wanted to scare you or kill you. Maybe he's worried you'll take some of his money. Maybe he didn't like the fact that you were nosing around his company and asking questions you shouldn't have been. Maybe he didn't like the fact that you went to a shareholders' meeting to meet him and ended up settling for me instead." David's voice rose and his expression turned angry. His words were tripping over themselves, and with so many contradictions in what he was saying now to what he had said before, I knew that he would be of no use. David didn't want to help me. He wanted to bed me.

"He told you about that?" I bit down on my lower lip. When had David realized that I'd gone to the shareholders' meeting to meet Mattias?

"Do you think I didn't know?" David's lips thinned. "Do you think I couldn't tell that you were more interested in meeting Mattias than actually dating me?"

"It wasn't like that, David." My breath caught. I'd never had any clue that David had been onto me. Not once. He'd hidden his knowledge well. I was starting to wonder what else he'd been hiding.

"It doesn't matter." His tone changed as the waiter walked back with our appetizers. "What's done is done."

"I didn't mean to use you."

"You didn't though, did you?" His expression changed. "You might be beautiful, Bianca, but your beauty isn't enough to make me lose my head."

I started then to realize that maybe David wasn't as innocent as he had let on. Maybe he'd spoken to Mattias and told him things that had made him kidnap me. Maybe after all this, it was really about the money. Maybe my perfect charade hadn't been so perfect after all.

"Shall we eat?" He nodded toward the food

My stomach churned. This was the last place I wanted to be right now. I'd made a mistake. Another big mistake. I shouldn't have come here. Now more than ever, I needed to speak to Larry. David wasn't going to lead me to Maxwell any more than he'd led me to Mattias. If history was any indicator, David would be on the phone to warn Maxwell that I was trying to find him. I needed to learn to be smarter. I needed to keep my mouth shut. I was wasting precious time and energy with David. Time I should have spent trying to figure out where Larry was. Larry was the man with the key to answers I needed. I'd been making fun of David's lack of detective skills, but maybe I was the one that was about to fail the academy.

# five

Dinner ended awkwardly, but I didn't care. I left the restaurant eagerly, but my journey home wasn't as satisfying as it used to be after a long night out. My home used to be my refuge, my comfort in good times and bad. Now it was just a place to rest my head. Even when all I wanted to do was walk into my apartment and head to my bed, I hesitated. My keys were in the lock, but I didn't want to turn them. Some part of me was scared to open the door. My body was on edge; the hairs on my arms standing at attention, the voice in the back of my head telling me to go somewhere else. My apartment was no longer the place I could seek solace. It was a place I wanted to hide from. It held too many secrets, had seen too many things. And I didn't feel safe there anymore. It doesn't matter how many doors I lock or how many windows I close, I know that someone can still get inside.

My fingers trembled on the keys, their grip tight but unwilling. I took a deep breath and shook my head, annoyed at myself for being so silly. Nothing was going to happen to me. Nothing at all. I opened the door and stepped inside quickly, shutting it behind me. Only two seconds later did I feel the hand on my mouth.

"Be quiet, Bianca," he whispered in my ear, and I froze, my body relaxing against my will, melting back into him and letting him know how much I'd missed him.

"Jakob?" I said finally as I turned around to face him.

His blue eyes were angry as he stared at me. "Why did you have dinner with David?"

"So much for the pleasantries," I grumbled. " 'How are you, Bianca?' 'I'm fine. How are you, Jakob?' 'I've been better.' 'Oh, me too.' "

"Stop muttering to yourself." He grunted, but I could see a hint of a smile on his face.

"What are you doing in my apartment? How did you get in here?" I glared at him. "And is this the first time you've been in here?"

"Tell me why you had dinner with David." He glared back at me and his eyes dropped to my lips. I couldn't stop myself from taking him in wholly. It hadn't been so long since I'd last seen him, but it felt like months and months.

"And you look so sexy," he growled. "Why?"

"Why do I look sexy?" I frowned at him, secretly thrilled that he'd called me sexy. I felt that my body was a traitor to the rest of me.

"Why did you go to dinner with David looking sexy?"

"You know I used to date him," I said childishly, looking for a reaction.

"And you said that was for a reason. You said you never had sex with him—or did you lie?"

"We didn't have sex, not that it's your business, but we also did more than nothing."

"Oh?" His eyes narrowed and he grabbed my wrists and pulled me toward him. "Did you do more than nothing tonight as well?"

"That's none of your business."

"Goddamnit, Bianca." His arms circled my waist and he peered down at me. "Why do you make this so fucking hard?" He pulled me into him as his lips came dangerously close to mine. His eyes were dark with desire.

"What do you think you're doing?" I gasped, my heart beating fast as my hands clutched his shoulders, not wanting to let go.

"What I should have done as soon as I saw you." His lips crashed down onto mine, taking possession and dominating as his tongue forced its way into my mouth. His lips took control of my tongue and sucked on it hard. My brain became mush as he filled my senses, completely overwhelming every internal protest trying to escape.

"Oh, Bianca," he muttered against my lips as his fingers played in my hair. "I haven't been able to get you out of my mind."

"Been thinking about me stopping the merger?" I responded churlishly as he sucked on my lower lip.

"No." His eyes met mine and his teeth bit down on my lip.

"Ouch! That hurt."

"You deserve to be punished. You didn't listen to me."

"Listen to you? About what?"

"I told you not to trust David."

"You mean your brother?" I snapped.

"Bianca, it's a long story."

"Isn't it always?"

"Stop being so . . ."

"So what?"

"Obstinate. Annoying. Childish." He glared. "And sexy."

"I'm afraid I can't stop that part." I winked at him.

He groaned, smiling at me for the first time. "I've missed you," he whispered, and sighed.

"I haven't missed you."

"Oh, Bianca, you always were a poor liar." He laughed as he held my face in his hands. "We need to talk."

"No, you need to tell me what you're doing here and how you got in."

"Like I said, we need to talk."

"*I* don't need to talk. I need *you* to talk and then leave."

"I'm not leaving." He glared at me.

"You're not staying."

"I want you."

"Is that meant to make me feel good?" I ignored the soft glow in my stomach that said if that was his intent, it had worked.

"It's not meant to make you feel any way. It's just a statement of fact."

"Okay, so you want me. And?"

"You want me too." He grinned as he looked down at my breasts, where I knew my nipples were poking out of my top.

"No, I don't." I glared at him, stopping myself from crossing my arms over my chest. "You have two minutes to talk and then I'm calling the cops."

"What did David say to you over dinner?"

"What?" I sighed, confused. "At what point? The point you were texting me or . . . ?"

"Bianca, this is important." He pursed his lips into a thin line; a nerve throbbing in his forehead told me he was serious.

"I don't get the two of you." I glared at him. "Why do you want to know what he said? Why did he want to know if I'd heard from you? If you guys are in on this together, why do you both act as if you don't trust each other? Is this all part of the game?"

"What did you say?" Jakob's eyes narrowed into slits as he gazed at me. He looked like a predator deciding whether he should eat his prey or wait for later.

"I said, why did he want to know if—"

"No, no, no—what did you say when he asked if you'd heard from me?"

"I said no." I frowned. "I'm not sure why, though. Why did he ask me that, and why do you care? Aren't the two of you in on this together?"

"Bianca, there's so much you need to know." He sighed. "But not now, not yet."

"Why won't you just tell me what's going on? You're killing me, Jakob!"

"Why do you still call me Jakob if you think I'm Mattias?" He smiled at me as his fingers ran down the side of my face.

"I don't know." I nibbled on my lower lip as his lips moved toward mine. "It would feel weird to call you Mattias."

"What do you know about Mattias, Bianca?"

"You mean, what do I know about you?" I made a face.

"Yes." He nodded and sighed. "Aside from what I told you on the island, what do you know?"

"I know that you're David's brother. I know that you're the CEO of Bradley Inc. I know you respect your privacy. I know that you never wanted to meet me for dinner when I was dating David. I know that you don't like to attend shareholders' meetings. I know that you have a great security team because there's nothing about you on the Web, not even a photo." I gazed at his handsome face. "Let me guess: You're scared that if people knew how rich you are and saw how hot you are, you'd have even more gold diggers than you have now?"

"And what you know about Mattias, you think that adds up to me? To who I am as a person? To the man you knew on the island? The man you made love to? The man who opened up to you? All of that adds up?"

"I don't know you, period." I shrugged. "I don't really know who you are. Everything you did and said was a lie."

"I want to take you in my arms and hold you and just stare at you until you realize that you do know me," he said with an intensity that I found both frightening and thrilling.

"We're strangers, Jakob. And I don't trust you. You don't know me either. If you did, you would know that—"

"It doesn't feel like we just met," he muttered against my lips. "It doesn't feel like I barely know you."

"What do you mean?"

"I've missed you." He kissed me softly, his eyes never leaving mine. "I've missed your taste."

"You can't just come into my apartment and . . ." I stepped back at his words, my face burning in shame. That was the second time tonight a Bradley brother had told me that he missed my taste. It made me feel slightly powerful, but, if I was honest with myself, a little cheap as well. I stared at his face and my stomach flipped as I studied his handsome features. I wanted to be with him. In fact, part of me believed that it would be helpful to give myself to him in every way. I'd have to be smart about it. I'd have to think with my head and not let my heart get in the way. At the end of the day, sex was just sex. Yes, I wanted him. Yes, there was a chemistry between us that took my breath away. However, I needed to control it. By sleeping with him, I would be telling him I trusted him again. If he thought I trusted him, he might let his guard down a bit more. And the more his guard was down, the more helpful he would be to me. I just had to make sure that I didn't let the sex take over everything. I had to make sure that I didn't let my body win. I knew that it would be hard to sleep with him without feeling like a bit of a slut, but I knew that I had to try and hide my disbelief as much as possible and make him believe that I still trusted him in a way. He'd played me, I had no problems or qualms in playing him now.

"Please, Bianca, don't you feel the need flowing between us? Don't you feel the heat and power?"

"It's just lust." I tried to pull away from him, but I couldn't. And I wasn't going to. Let him think that all I needed was his heat and hardness.

"I would never hurt you, Bianca." He bit down on my lower lip and sucked. "I didn't lie to you on the island."

"You told me you didn't know Mattias. You said you'd never met him. You didn't let on that David was your brother either. Wouldn't that have been a fun fact?" I said and sucked on his lower lip, playing my role well. " 'Ooh, guess what, Bianca? That guy you dated, well, he's my brother.' "

"How could I have told you David was my brother? When would have been the right time for that?" Jakob kissed me hard, making it impossible for me to respond. Mentally I knew that there would have been no good time. If I'd known whom I was with, I would have panicked, perhaps run into the jungle. Maybe I'd still be stuck on the island, lost somewhere. "There are so many things you don't know,

Bianca. When we arrived on the island, I had one thought in my mind, and that was to find out the truth about you and your family. I wanted to exact revenge for—"

"You wanted to 'exact revenge' on me?" My jaw dropped. "Is this a bad joke? You think you can come and tell me you wanted revenge on me while you try and seduce me on the side? How stupid do you think I am?" My voice was loud and I tried to control it. I didn't want him to see just how disdainful I was of his responses.

"Bianca, there are things in our parents' pasts. There are things that your mother did and your father did that cannot be changed. Things that ruined people's lives. I just wanted to get to the bottom of it all."

"And you think I should pay for that?" I froze as I remembered something he'd once told me. "Was that why you said something about children paying for the sins of their fathers?"

"That's how life goes, Bianca." He grabbed my shoulders. "But I was wrong to play God. I was wrong to just believe—"

"Believe what?" I cut him off angrily. "What do you believe?"

"I believe that I want to touch you." He fingers pressed into my skin. "I believe that every night since we've been apart, I've craved your touch. I've gone crazy thinking about what I did to you. You have to believe that I . . ." He grabbed my face. "Look at me, Bianca. I need you to look at me."

"Why? Why should I believe you? What have you done

for me that should make me trust you? You're in my fucking apartment, Jakob. How did you get in here? You're still sending me freaking messages trying to scare me."

"What?" He shook his head and his eyes narrowed. "I haven't sent you any messages."

"And you changed your name on your letter from Jakob to Mattias."

"What?" He froze, his blue eyes taking on a fiery light. "I didn't change anything."

"Then who?" I shrugged. "You're the only one who seems to be watching me and breaking into my apartment like some sort of stalker."

"I'm trying to protect you."

"Protect me from what? I don't need protection from anyone but you." I pushed him away from me. "I want you to leave. Now."

"You don't want me to leave."

"Yes, I do."

"Do you still not trust me, Bianca? After everything? After I let you go?"

"Why *did* you let me go? After all that? Why?" I implored him. "I just want to understand." My entire body was tense as I waited for a response. *Calm down, Bianca*, I lectured myself inwardly. *Be cool, sexy, intriguing. Don't be that girl. I can't be that girl, if I want my plan to work.*

"I promise I will tell you everything soon." He walked toward the window and looked out. "You should close your curtains. Anyone can look in here." He turned toward me, his brows furrowed. “You look very sexy. Did you dress up for David?”

“I dressed up for me.”

“Not a look I’m used to seeing on you.” He smiled. “I miss the messy hair and dirt-streaked face.”

“Whatever.”

“I miss watching you walking around in my shirt, your cute little ass playing hide-and-seek with me.” He took a step toward me. “I miss you sleeping curled up next to me, playing with my cock in your sleep.”

“Jakob.” I stared at him, mesmerized by the look in his eyes as he stopped in front of me. “No.” I said it softly, my hand touching his and then falling to the side.

“I miss the feel of your skin against mine.” His hand dropped to my leg and I felt his fingers running up the inside of my trembling thigh. He took another step toward me and kissed me lightly. “I miss every part of you, Bianca. Every single part of you.” He kissed me gently at first and I couldn’t stop myself from kissing him back. Oh, how I’d missed the feel of his lips against mine. How I’d missed the gentle roughness of his fingers as he caressed my skin. *Focus, Bianca,* I commanded myself. *Have some fun, but remember the ulterior motive and goal. You want him to think you’re putty in his hands. You want him to think the sex is so good that you just can’t resist him. You want him to think all he has to do is touch you and everything will be okay. That’s how you’ll get some power and information.* A part of me felt dirty for playing the game, but the other part of me felt high on life. Why shouldn’t I be pleasured while I played him? Men did it to women all the time.

"Oh," I moaned as his hands cupped my breasts through my dress.

"I need you," he groaned, and I felt his fingers gently sliding my dress straps off my shoulders. I couldn't resist him, I didn't want to. My fingers found their way to his shirt and I unbuttoned it quickly, pulling it open so that I could touch his chest. He groaned as my fingers made contact with his skin and I stood still as he pulled my dress off. "So beautiful," he muttered as he gazed at me in my bra and panties. I felt his fingers undoing my bra, and before I knew it, that too was on the ground. I closed my eyes as his fingers played with my nipples roughly, his hands cupping and caressing my breasts. Lowering his head, he took my right nipple in his mouth and sucked hard, and a spasm of ecstasy ran through my body. All I could think about was the feelings of pleasure dancing around in the pit of my stomach as he took my hands and guided me to my bedroom. We said nothing as we stood next to the bed, just staring at each other. All of the fears I'd felt on the balcony were gone. All I could think about was that I was here with this man. This man that I craved so badly that I wanted to dismiss all of my doubts.

"Don't think," he whispered as he picked me up and placed me on the bed before jumping up himself. His fingers ran down my stomach lightly, teasing me as they inched toward my panties. My body anxiously awaited the moment that he would touch me there and reawaken the flower. He didn't leave me waiting long. His fingers slipped inside my panties eagerly, rubbing my wetness as he sucked on my earlobe. My toes curled as my body shifted slightly to give him more access. He slipped my panties off quickly and my fingers found my way to his hardness within seconds of his leaning back onto the bed next to me. I moaned as my fingers moved up and down on his girth, teasing and taunting him. The tip of his cock was wet with anticipation and he grunted as my fingers gripped him firmly. He pushed me back down and lowered himself onto me, his eyes never leaving my face as he guided his hardness inside me. I cried out as he entered me slowly, allowing me to feel every inch of him as he filled me up. My walls closed in on him, welcoming him home, and his body shook as he increased his pace. He grabbed my hands and moved them up next to my head as he increased his pace, his cock entering me quickly and urgently. My breasts bounced against his chest as he entered me and the hairs on his chest tickled my nipples and teased them even more.

"Oh, Bianca," he grunted as I wrapped my legs around his waist and he leaned down to kiss me, his tongue entering my mouth in rhythm with his cock. I sucked on his tongue as I felt my body quivering beneath him; my fingers scratched his back and played with his hair, and his smell drove me crazy. Pulling back slightly, he grabbed my legs and put them over his shoulders as he increased his pace even faster. I closed my eyes, unable to stop myself from screaming as my orgasm built up.

"Look at me," he commanded as his fingers rubbed my

clit roughly while he continued to enter me. "I want to see you when you come for me."

"Jakob," I moaned, feeling feverish. "Oh!" I screamed as I found myself coming hard. "Oh," I cried out again as his finger continued to rub me.

"Oh, Bianca." He slammed into me one last time and pulled out quickly as he exploded onto my stomach. "Oh, Bianca." He leaned back down and kissed me hard. "How I've missed you. I never should have let you go," he muttered in my ear as his fingers played with my nipples.

I lay back, body heaving and brain racing dangerously close to the brink of insanity. All of a sudden, I was feeling panicky. Was I really ready to play this game? It didn't feel like a game anymore. It didn't feel like I was in control. The endorphins that had taken over my brain and led me to sleeping with Jakob once again were leaving faster than they'd arrived, and I felt as if I were in bed with the enemy. An enemy my body didn't want to acknowledge existed. My brain, though, couldn't forget that Jakob was Mattias and he was playing a game with me. A dangerous game, and if I wasn't careful, I would never win.

"You give me fever." He grabbed my hand and held it to his forehead. "Being with you gives me fever like I've never felt before."

"Isn't that a song?" I whispered as I gazed into his eyes, my body instantly wanting to trust him again, but my brain reminding me to stay on track. I was doing this for a reason. I could control my heart and my body as long as I focused.

"I don't know. Is it?" He brought my hand down to his lips and kissed it lightly.

"We need to talk, Jakob." I rolled over. "I want the truth."

"All I want is to flip you upside down and take you again." He fingers played with my belly button and then he jumped out of the bed. "I need to use the restroom."

"Okay." I nodded and stared at his tight butt as he walked across the room. My body started trembling as I lay there, and not from sexual excitement. This was wrong on so many levels. I was confused on so many levels. Staring at a naked Jakob was heaven and hell, and I didn't know if he was an angel here to save me or a devil waiting to pull me into the pit of fire.

"I'll be right back." He opened the door. "And then we can get back to business."

"One thing first: How did you get into my apartment?"

"I have a key." He closed the door.

And I took a deep breath and made my decision.

# six

No one will ever say I should go to the Olympics. I'm not someone who could win a hundred-meter dash, but as soon as Jakob went into the bathroom, I jumped out of bed so quickly that I'd have given Usain Bolt a run for his money. I wedged my desk chair in front of the bathroom door, threw on some sweatpants, a shirt, and a jacket, grabbed my handbag and phone, and ran out the door. I didn't want to leave. My body was still trembling in remembrance of the magic it had just experienced, but I was more confused than ever.

I didn't trust myself around Jakob. He hadn't told me anything new, yet I hadn't been able to resist him. I was putty in his hands. For all I knew, this was part of his game. Maybe this was why he'd let me go. He wanted me to trust him. He wanted me to think that I had nothing to fear from him. Maybe he was conditioning me so that he could gain my trust and get what he was really after. The problem was, I didn't know what he was really after and I was beginning to fall under his spell again; not that I was sure I'd ever left it. I needed to be stronger than this. This had to be the last mistake I made trusting him—and sleeping with him. I couldn't afford to let my heart lead me anymore.

I ran out of the building and into the street, hurrying into a crowd of people. All of a sudden sadness crept into my soul. I didn't feel as if I'd made the right move, but I knew staying wouldn't have been right either. The grief inside me had become an empty void. My stomach growled, but I wasn't hungry. I didn't want to continue on this journey, but I felt like it was too late to turn back. I was being played and also trying to play my own games and I was so caught up that I didn't know what way was right any more. My weakness for Jakob was only going to make everything more difficult. I'd started this journey by myself and I needed to rely on myself. That look in his eyes, in David's—that wasn't love, that wasn't adoration. It was lust and desire. And lust and desire were cheap and commonplace emotions. If I was going to continue searching for the truth, I needed to be stronger, harder, more focused. And I needed to figure out exactly how far I was willing to go. I'd already crossed a line I'd never thought I'd cross when I'd calculatingly slept with Jakob. I needed to make sure that whatever decisions I made moving forward were going to be ones I could live with.

I pulled out my phone and called the only person I could. The only person who could advise me without having an agenda.

"Hey, Bianca," Rosie answered on the second ring. "Where are you?"

"Walking down the street. Want to get a drink?"

"Oh, I would, but I still have my date tonight."

"Oh, right." I wanted to ask Rosie if her date was more like a booty call, but I didn't want to be rude.

"I can cancel though, if you need me."

"No, no, don't cancel. When am I going to meet him?" I asked softly.

"Soon, I hope." Rosie sighed. "We had a bit of an argument. I'm not sure it's going to work out. We're meeting late tonight to discuss the future of our relationship."

"Oh no, why?"

"You know me, I have trust issues." She sounded short. "He isn't like most guys."

"Oh?"

"Well, he's rich and powerful and he doesn't like to listen to women." She paused. "Though of course he listens to me."

"As he should." *He sounds like an asshole already.*

"Where are you?" Rosie sounded confused. "Where have you been?"

"I'm taking a walk. I think I'll go to the university library."

"Oh, why?"

"Research."

"On what? Did you speak to Larry Renee again?"

"No, I didn't. He . . ." I paused.

"He what?" she asked, sounding very interested in my answer.

"He didn't have much to say the first time we spoke."

"Oh, that's good."

"That's good?"

"I mean it's good that there's not more craziness going on. It's good that you know all there is to know."

"Yeah, but do I? What do I really know?" My voice rose as I crossed the street, dodging a yellow cab as I jaywalked. "Screw you too!" I shouted back at the driver.

"What's going on, Bianca?" Rosie sounded anxious. "Are you sure you don't want me to cancel? I totally wouldn't mind."

"Rosie, no, you can't cancel. I won't let you. Have your talk with your guy and I'll see you tomorrow."

"I'm worried about you, Bianca. You haven't been the same since your dad died."

"That's what happens when you lose a parent."

"Yes, I suppose it is." Rosie's voice was a monotone. "I guess I don't know what that's like. I don't remember my dad, and, well, my mom is still around."

"It's hard." I sighed. "I wish now that I'd asked more questions. I wish I knew more about his past. I wish I'd tried to reach him on a deeper level instead of just accepting that he was depressed over my mother's death."

"I suppose he felt guilty."

"You think so?"

"I mean it was his fault, right?"

"What do you mean?"

"I don't know. I guess most people blame themselves when a loved one dies."

"Yeah, it was like he died while he was still alive." Tears rolled down my face as I walked aimlessly, no longer caring where I was going.

"I guess that's what happens when you love too hard. You become broken when you lose them."

"I never want to love that hard."

"Me either." Rosie's voice was strong. "I'm not going to let any man ruin my life."

"It's hard though, isn't it? It's hard not to let someone get too close."

"You really liked Mattias, didn't you?"

"Yeah." I gulped. "I really did."

"Have you heard from him since you've been back?"

"No." I stopped outside a bodega.

"Do you want to see him?"

"I want answers, so maybe."

"That's not the right answer, Bianca. You can't see him! Who knows what he'd do? Especially if he still wants something from you. Especially if you don't want to go to the police."

"I just don't know what I'd say to the police," I whispered into the phone. "Would they even believe me?"

"I don't know, Bianca. I don't know what you'd tell them. Mattias Bradley, the CEO of one of the biggest corporations in the world, kidnapped me and then flew me home and I don't know why."

"Yeah." I closed my eyes. "They'd laugh me out of the

precinct." I took a deep breath. "Hey, I'm about to head into the subway. I'll call you later, okay?"

"Okay. I'll see you tomorrow, Bianca. Stay safe."

I hung up the phone, my heart pounding as I tried to figure out what to do next. I couldn't go home, not with Jakob there—and not with his having a key. I'd have to get the locks changed. I didn't know what he was thinking, but I knew that he'd be angry that I'd escaped. I was in a maze and had no idea how to get out. The events of the past week were leading me in one direction, but all I could see were the walls. There still seemed to be no clear path out of this mess. I was angry and upset and so, so sad. I had nowhere to go and no one to talk to. I was all alone. I missed my dad. I mean *really* missed him. And more than that, I missed the lost opportunities that I had had with him.

I'd never fought for a better relationship. I'd never tried to cross that line to have a deeper, more significant relationship with him. I'd accepted his pain and lived with it. I'd occupied my mind with other things. Felt love and acceptance in other ways. I'd experienced the love of a father in movies. I'd experienced the childhood I'd always wanted by watching *Meet Me in St. Louis.* I had been Judy Garland, I had the caring and protective parents, the wonderful sisters, the next-door neighbor that made my heart clamor, I was on the trolley singing about the ringing and the dinging of the bell. I was happy in those moments. I was a part of something. That was the life I'd grown up with. It wasn't real and it wasn't mine, but I felt the heartache and the love and it was as if it were mine. It had been enough. Just like my favorite book, *Homecoming*, by Cynthia Voigt. I'd read that book every year since I was ten years old. The sadness and the loneliness of the Tillerman children was my own, and while I didn't have the siblings, I had the feelings. I was on that journey, looking for home. I'd always been on that journey. I'd just never acknowledged it.

"Hey, girl, you okay?" An old black man standing by a trash can looked at me with wide eyes.

"I'm fine, thank you."

"You homeless?" He looked at me knowingly.

"No." I shook my head.

"Don't let them boys up at the corner recruit you." He reached into his pocket. "It ain't the way. Don't get in no strange cars."

"I'm not going to get into any strange cars."

"Them men be sick. Some of them look sane, but, girl, they be sick."

"Yes, sir."

"You too good a girl to become a prostitute."

"I'm not going to become a prostitute, sir." I wiped the tears from my eyes and tried not to laugh.

"Why you crying?" He handed me some gum. "You wanna piece?"

"No thanks." I shook my head, but he kept his hand held out, so I took a piece. "Thank you."

"It's Juicy Fruit." He grinned. "Juicy Fruit always makes you feel better."

"Thank you." I unwrapped the paper and started to chew it. The sweetness of the gum invaded my shroud of sadness and I started to feel a bit more like myself again.

"It's a cold world out there." He looked up and down the street. "Look around you, girl, all these people with all this money, but who's really happy?"

"I don't know." I shrugged and looked around me. People were walking quickly in their suits, looking important and just as lonely as me.

"Everyone got somewhere to go. Somewhere to be. Everyone's in a hurry, but you know what? When they get home, there's no one there waiting. There's no one there caring. All that money, all that power, it don't mean nothing in the end."

"But people will do anything for money." My voice cracked. "They'll even kill people."

"You got some loan sharks after you?" He frowned. "You got the Mafia on your tail?"

"Oh no, nothing like that."

"Them people ain't no good. They'll kill you or cut off your hand to make an example of you."

"I don't have the Mafia after me." I gave him a big smile and wiped my eyes. My tears had completely dried up.

"Your boyfriend just break up with you?"

"I don't have a boyfriend." I shook my head. "There's a guy I like, but I don't know . . ." *Why did I say that?*

"Let me give you some advice, girl. If he's for you, if he loves you, he'll show you. Don't chase no man."

"He kidnapped me."

"He what?" His eyes widened again. "He don't sound like the man for you."

"It's a long story." I sighed. "I don't even know what to believe anymore."

"I'm going to give you some advice." He came closer to me. "The truth is never what you expect. Go back to the beginning. Go sit somewhere quiet and think about everything. Look up at the stars or the moon and just think. The answers will come."

"I don't know if the answers will come just like that. This situation is complicated." I wished it were that easy, but I was pretty sure I'd need to be high on mushrooms or something for the answers to come from the sky.

"Life is as complicated as we make it, child. You believe in God?"

"I don't know." I bit my lower lip, feeling guilty and ashamed. "I think so."

"Girl, you go pray to God for some guidance and answers. He'll put you on the right path."

"Thank you, I'll do that." I smiled at him. "Thank you for talking to me. You've made me feel better."

"We all in this together, girl."

"Thank you." I smiled at him again and turned to go down the street. "I really needed to talk to someone tonight."

"Anytime, girl. I'm here every day." He grinned and nodded toward the pile of clothes next to me. My heart caught as I realized he lived here. He lived in the street. He was homeless. "You need any money?" He pulled some dollars out of his pocket and handed them to me. "It's not much, but it's all I have."

"Oh no, I couldn't." I was horrified and touched by his offer. "No, thank you, though. Thank you and God bless you."

"We all got to look out for each other, girl." He looked at me thoughtfully. "You ain't never alone, remember that."

"Thank you." I gave him a quick hug. "Thank you. Sometimes I feel like I'm all by myself, but you've made me remember that I can't just dwell on my sorrow and regrets."

"It ain't worth it." His eyes crinkled at me. "Trust me, girl. It ain't worth it."

"You'll have to tell me your story one day."

"Henry." He gave me a small bow.

"I'm Bianca, Henry."

"Good to meet you, Miss Bianca." He grinned. "Now you get you home before some not-so-nice guy tries to take advantage of your big brown eyes."

"I'm going to come back." I stared at him. "I'm going to come back to see you." *And bring you some money when I have it.*

"I look forward to it."

I walked back down the street away from Henry, feeling a different kind of sadness. For once, my thoughts weren't on myself. For once, I was reminded that a whole big world was out there and I was still a part of it. The world didn't revolve around the Bradley brothers and their drama. It didn't even revolve around my father and his inventions or my mother's death. I could move on and just forget about it. Only I knew I couldn't. Not after everything. I needed answers. I needed to find Larry.

Beep beep.

*Where are you?*

*I had to leave.*

*And lock me in?*

*Sorry.*

*I could have left.*

*I didn't want you to try and convince me to let you stay.*

*I'm leaving now so you can come home.*

*I don't trust you.*

*I'm the most trustworthy person you know.*

*Says the kidnapper.*

*Don't trust anyone, Bianca. Don't talk to David.*

*I don't and I won't.*

*Tell me where you are. There are some things you should know. This is for your own good.*

*No thanks. I don't trust you.*

*You can trust me. It's the others you shouldn't trust.*

*Why should I trust you?*

*I was just in your bed.*

*Sex doesn't equal trust.*

*Methinks someone wants me back in her bed.*

*Methinks you have the wrong century, Shakespeare.*

*Did Shakespeare coin* methinks*?*

*Jakob.*

*I like it when you text my name, though I prefer when you scream it.*

*I'm surprised you haven't asked me to call you Mattias.*

*Tyler Durden.*

*Huh?*

*Figure it out.*

*Figure what out? Tyler Durden from* Fight Club*? What does that have to do with anything?*

*What I told you before is true.*

*What are you talking about?*

*You watch movies right?*

*Yes, so what?*

*Figure out Tyler. It's the only clue I can give you for now. And even that's too much.*

*So what did you tell me?*

*I told you your mom wasn't an innocent.*

His next text was a photograph of a woman and man in bed, naked and laughing. They looked wild and illicit.

*What is this?* I texted back as my phone let out a warning beep.

*My dad and your mom.* Just as his last text arrived, my phone died. I bit down on my lower lip as I tried to picture the lady's face in the photo. I was almost positive that wasn't my mom. Why did he think it was? Did he blame my mom for his father's cheating and making his mother unhappy? Was this what all of this had been about after all? I had no idea who the lady in the photo was, and now my phone was dead and I couldn't even let him know.

I realized then that he really did think that my mom had slept with his dad. Someone had to have put that in his head, someone who wanted to pit us against each other. The woman in the photo was not my mom, but he seemed convinced it was her. Had David told him that? And if so, why? I needed to talk to Larry right away. I was going to have to help his wife locate him.

Now was the time for me to start getting the answers I needed. A ray of hope flickered in my heart. Maybe Jakob wasn't so bad after all. Someone else was orchestrating these lies, but I didn't know who or why. I needed to find out what was going on, but now it was for more than just my parents. It was for my relationship with Jakob as well.

~

The good thing about staying in cheap hotels is that they always have a Yellow Pages. I stared at the address that I'd scribbled on a scrap of paper and smiled. The address had matched up with the phone number I'd called for Larry. This had to be right.

"Will you need me to wait for you?" the cabdriver asked as he drove down the long, tree-lined street in Syosset.

"No, I'll be fine. Thank you." I shook my head and ignored the doubt that had crept into my mind. I didn't even know if Mrs. Renee would be home or if she would see me, but there was no way I could pay the waiting fee for the cab.

I didn't have much money left and I had to stretch what I had. I couldn't afford to be taking so many taxi rides after this; not until I started working again. This had been an extravagance I'd allowed myself because of my eagerness to see Mrs. Renee, but I couldn't afford to spend all my cash on transportation.

"You live out here? It's a nice place."

"No, I'm visiting a friend."

"It's one of the nicer parts of Long Island." We drove past huge houses. "I'm a Staten Island guy myself."

"That's nice," I said politely.

"Not really, but that's where my family is. If I could afford it, I'd move to a big high-rise on Park Avenue with a doorman and all that shit."

"You and me both." I laughed.

"Yeah, but what we going to do?" He laughed. "People just gotta make do."

"Yeah." I sat back and looked out the window, feeling slightly put out. I couldn't afford to live on Park Avenue or in a building with a doorman, but maybe I would have been living that lifestyle if Jeremiah Bradley hadn't ripped off my dad's inventions.

"We can't all be Donald Trump." The driver chuckled. "If you don't have billions like The Donald, you're just a schmuck in New York."

"I guess we're both schmucks, then." I laughed and tried to ignore the feeling of entitlement that had coursed through me at his words. Maybe I wasn't meant to be a schmuck like him. Maybe my father was meant to have riches like Donald Trump. Maybe the cabdriver was assuming things he knew nothing about. I sighed as I felt myself becoming riled up. Maybe I was being oversensitive . . .

"This is it." He pulled up a long driveway to a house that looked like a miniversion of the White House. "Your friend has a lot of money."

"More money than I thought." I handed him some twenties and got out of the car. "Keep the change."

"Thanks." He grinned as he backed out. "Have a fun time."

"I'll try," I mumbled as I watched him back out of the driveway and walked to the front door. This was it, then. In all the years I'd known Larry, I'd never thought he was rich. I'd only seen him a few times. I'd never gotten the feeling that he was super successful. I rang the doorbell and waited. And waited. Then I rang the doorbell again. I took a few steps back and looked up at the house. The curtain at a window on the right side of the house moved slightly and I walked back to the door and banged hard.

"Mrs. Renee, it's me, Bianca London. Please open up," I said loudly as I banged and rang the doorbell again. A few seconds later the door opened slightly.

"You shouldn't be here." Her voice sounded panicked.

"Please, Mrs. Renee, I need to talk to you."

"You need to leave, Bianca." She made to close the door again and I pushed against it.

"Please, I won't stay long. I just need to talk to you." I pushed the door harder. "I'm not leaving until we talk."

"Come in, then." She opened the door a few more inches and I stepped in swiftly before she slammed it shut again. I stared at her small, worried figure and frowned. She looked as if she'd just seen a ghost. Her white hair looked unkempt and she was wearing a dirty white blouse with a pair of black sweats.

"Have you heard from Larry?" I asked her softly, looking around the dark hallway as we stood there.

She nodded, her eyes huge as she stared at me. "He's in hiding."

"So he wasn't kidnapped?"

"No." She shook her head. "What do you want?"

"I need to speak to him. I need him to explain what he meant about the papers he gave me. I need to understand the clues."

"I'm sorry, but that won't be possible." She shook her head. "He can't help you anymore."

"Why is he so scared? Who is he scared of?"

"They're not good people. He's a monster."

"Who's a monster?" I took a step toward her. "Who's a monster?"

"You need to leave, Bianca. They know you're here. They know everything. I can't say anything. If I do, he'll know. He'll know and he'll kill me and Larry."

"What do you know that they will kill you about?" I grabbed her arms. "What is going on here?"

"It wasn't meant to be like this." She shook her head. "Larry didn't know, not in the beginning. He thought they were good people, but they were all bad. They'll ruin Larry if he says anything. That's not right. He didn't know, he really didn't know."

"What didn't he know?"

"This isn't your fight, Bianca. Leave this place. Leave New York. Go anywhere, anywhere else in the world. You don't have to let them manipulate you."

"The papers that Larry gave me, they said that my father was a rightful partner in Bradley Inc. Many of the patents were in his name. When did he give away his rights? Or did he even give them away?"

Her face was still as she contemplated my face. "I don't know what you're talking about. Your dad didn't give any of his rights away." She walked down the hallway and into the kitchen. I followed her and watched as she picked up a pen and a pad of paper. "Would you like a drink? Some tea perhaps?" she asked me softly, and scribbled something down and held it up: *They hear everything.*

"Tea would be fine, thanks." I frowned and watched as she scribbled something else, motioning me over to look at the notepad.

*They have already threatened to kill us.*

"Who?" I asked, then slapped my mouth. "Who are you going to . . ." My voice trailed off as she frowned at me and handed me the pen and paper. I scribbled quickly, *Who is threatening you? The Bradleys?*

She shook her head vehemently and pursed her lips before turning around and turning the kettle on. "Would you like milk and sugar?" she asked brightly.

"Sure."

"How many?"

"A little milk and two sugars please." I didn't hide my impatience well.

"Okay." She took some cups from the cupboard and then scribbled down something else. *The last threat I received was from Maxwell's wife.*

"What?" My jaw dropped and my mind was racing. Maxwell's wife. Everything seemed to go back to the mysterious Maxwells. I grabbed the pen and paper and wrote quickly, *I need to talk to Larry*—NOW. I showed her the paper and she shook her head, her face going white.

"We have to get to the bottom of this," I whispered in her ear. "Or it's never going to end."

"I can't," she whispered urgently. "He can't talk to you."

"I was kidnapped and lied to. I need to know why. Larry owes me this. And my father. My father trusted him."

She looked up at me and I could see the worry in the lines of her face before she covered her eyes with her leathery, trembling fingers. I touched her arm and was surprised by how cold she was.

"Please, Mrs. Renee. It's the only option we have. If Larry doesn't talk to me, I can't help him. I can't solve this mystery and you can't go back to your previous existence. Let me speak to him."

She remained silent for seconds that felt like days as I waited. Finally, she nodded her head, as though she'd won an internal argument with herself.

"Not here." She took a deep breath. "It won't be safe here."

# seven

We sat in the diner in a corner booth and I stared at the pay phone next to the toilets.

"This is why I love Yelp." I smiled at her. "All I did is type in *pay phones* and I found this place."

"I didn't know they even had pay phones anymore." Mrs. Renee looked at me bleakly as she nibbled on her toast.

"They won't have tapped the pay phone." I leaned forward. "But if they're watching us, they will know we're up to something. I need to call and speak to him now."

"He won't like it." She looked nervous.

"He might not like it, but how long can he stay in hiding? How long can I sit around and wait to see what's going to happen to me next? I was kidnapped and I don't know why. I'm sleeping with a man I don't . . ." I sighed. "I don't want to get into all the details. Please just give me the phone number."

"No." She shook her head. "I'll call it and you can talk to him, but I'm not giving you the number."

"Fine." I nodded eagerly and handed her some quarters. "Here you go."

She took them from me and walked to the pay phone, looking behind her as she picked up the phone and quickly dialed. I watched as she talked into the phone and then waved me over.

I jumped up quickly and grabbed the phone from her. "Uncle Larry, it's Bianca."

"You shouldn't be calling me, Bianca." He sounded old and worried.

"They kidnapped me, Larry. They drugged me and kidnapped me. I deserve to know what's going on."

"You shouldn't have gone to that shareholders' meeting. I never should have gotten you that proxy access."

"Why? What are they afraid of?"

"I'm sorry, Bianca. I'm responsible for a huge lie."

"What huge lie? Did you know that Mattias was going to pretend to be Jakob and—"

"You met Jakob?" he cut me off, his voice keen.

"Yes, he's the one who kidnapped me. David told him I was looking for Mattias. He's Mattias, he—"

"Listen to me, Bianca, forget about Mattias Bradley."

"How am I supposed to forget—"

"The clues lead you past Mattias Bradley."

"What do you mean?"

"Mattias Bradley means nothing. He can't and won't hurt you."

"I don't understand, Larry."

"Mr. Bradley senior, he knew what he was doing, Bianca. We all knew what he was doing. It was a game in the beginning. All of us thought it was a game, me, your father, Bradley, Maxwell. And then Bradley started cheating on his wife and things got complicated. It was okay at first, it was just random women—but then it was Maxwell's wife and that's when everything changed."

"What do you mean?"

"That ruined everything."

"I don't understand."

"None of us were innocent, Bianca." His voice was lowered. "We all did things we shouldn't have; even your father."

"What did my father do?"

"You have a sibling, Bianca." Larry's voice dropped.

*"What?"* I shook my head in confusion. "No, that's impossible. I'm an only child."

"You have a sibling."

"I don't understand." My head felt heavy as I stared at the phone. "How is that possible?"

"Your dad had another child."

"What?" My voice rose. "No, he can't have. He never told me he had another child."

"He didn't find out until later." Larry's voice dropped. "There are things you don't know, Bianca. Things you shouldn't know. You need to just drop whatever it is you're doing. Your father made a huge mistake. One that he paid for dearly."

"What do you know, Uncle Larry?" I leaned forward, my heart beating rapidly as I gripped the phone. "You need to tell me."

"I've already told you too much."

"How is this all linked? Why are you hiding? What do you know?" I paused. "Are they scared that I want money? Do I have a brother or a sister?" I rambled on, my mind whirling with a million questions.

"This isn't about money. There are things you don't know. Things that certain people will do anything to keep private."

"And you know these secrets?"

"I know some of them. I don't know enough. I had hoped you could find out. You need to look at the paperwork I gave you again. There's something in there—" The phone went dead.

"Larry?" I asked frantically. "Larry?" I looked at his wife. "You need to call him back. The phone went dead. Call him back!"

She grabbed the phone, her face white as she dialed the numbers again. "It's disconnected." The fear in her eyes was impenetrable.

"Try it again, that can't be right," I demanded, and watched as she pressed the numbers.

"It says the number you're trying to call is no longer in service." Her voice cracked and she looked at me in hatred. "What have you done, Bianca? What have you done?"

# eight

"Pick up the phone, pick up the phone," I mumbled to myself as I listened to the ringing tones. "Come on, Rosie."

"Hello." Her voice was soft. "Bianca? Is everything okay?"

"No." I gulped. "It's really not."

"Where are you? What's wrong?"

"I'm in Riverside Park. I'm sitting on a park bench across from two elderly men and I think I'm about to lose it."

"Why? What happened?"

"I spoke to Larry, my father's attorney. He went into hiding because he's scared of the Bradley brothers. He thinks they're going to kill him. I'm not sure why. And he told me . . . I have a sibling."

"What?" Rosie sounded shocked. "But you're an only child."

"What if my mom really did have an affair and gave the child up?" I closed my eyes. "Oh my God, I can't even believe I said that. What is this craziness?"

"I'm going to come and see you. Where in Riverside Park? What cross streets?"

"No, don't come. I need to go find a locksmith so I can get my locks changed."

"Why are you changing your locks?"

"Seems like the smartest thing to do. Too many people seem to have access to my apartment."

"I don't even know what to say, Bianca. It sounds like a bad dream or some sort of thriller movie."

"Actually I feel like I'm in an episode of that new TV show *Stalker*. Only every week the focus is on me."

"Mattias Bradley must really want you to keep your hands off of the family company."

"Yeah, him or David. Or maybe even someone else."

"Someone else?"

"I think someone else is involved. It doesn't make sense that David and Jakob would be warning me away from each other if they were working together."

"Well, out of the two, David seems the most trustworthy. He isn't the one that kidnapped you."

"Yeah, you would think that would make me trust him more, but for some reason it makes me trust him less. In fact, I think I'm going to talk to Jakob. I'm going to let him explain what happened."

"Are you crazy? He kidnapped you."

"And he let me go. Yeah, maybe this is part of the trap. Maybe he let me go so that I would trust him again. I don't know if I trust him, but I do know that between him and David I trust him more."

"Girl, that doesn't even make sense. Let me come get you. Tell me everything Larry said and we'll see what we can figure out together."

"Thanks, I . . ." Beep beep. "Rosie, I have to go. I'm getting a call from the history department."

"Oh, okay. Do you want to meet up later?"

"I'll let you know," I said quickly, then answered the other line. "Hello?"

"Bianca London, is that you? It's Blake!" His voice was cheery and I couldn't stop myself from smiling. I was surprised to hear the sound of my old friend's voice, but oh so grateful.

"Blake, it's so good to hear from you!"

"You too, stranger." I could hear in his tone that he wasn't joking. "I've been calling you for ages. What's going on? I go to France for a few semesters to do some research, and when I come back, you've dropped out of the program and won't return my calls."

"Oh, Blake, it wasn't personal. You know that, right?" I sighed. "I'm sorry I haven't called."

"Yeah, I kinda expect my friends to call me back, maybe that's old-fashioned of me?"

"Don't be a doofus." I sighed.

"I thought you were mad because I asked you out before I went away. I didn't mean to pressure you."

"Blake, my dad died—and some really weird stuff has been happening."

"Oh yeah? Weird how?"

"You wouldn't believe me even if I told you." I sighed again.

"I'm a history major and I just got back from France with so many ghost stories that I could put the SyFy channel out of business. Trust me, I'd believe whatever you told me."

"How was France? And what ghost stories?" I laughed, confused by his admission.

"Lots of farmhouses in the suburbs of Paris were used to hide Jews from the Nazis. Lots of Jews and soldiers died, and, well, let's just say their spirits haven't quite moved on."

"No way. Are you serious?" My jaw dropped. "You saw a ghost?"

"Let's just say I heard a lot of stories and had one experience that has led me to say never say never."

"Wow."

"But enough about me. I want to hear about you and all these strange stories? Maybe I can help."

"I don't think so," I said regretfully. I didn't want to bring anyone else into my crazy life, least of all Blake. Blake was my first friend in the history program, and everything had been great until he'd made a move on me. I just hadn't liked him that way.

"Bianca, you know I'm here if you need to chat. I'm more than just my good looks. I've got a brain as well."

"Yes, that's true." I stared at the Hudson River in front of me and decided to go with my gut. "I do need someone to talk to, if you're up for that. Just trust me when I say it's a whole heap of crazy."

"I love crazy." He laughed. "Napoléon is my hero."

"And I'm guessing that's not Napoleon Dynamite."

"Bonaparte all the way, baby." He laughed. "But seriously, I have a bit of a break now, if you want to meet up for a coffee."

"I'm in Riverside Park." I stood up and started walking. "I should really be getting home, though. I need to find a locksmith to change my locks."

"Where in Riverside? I'm at One Hundred and Sixteenth Street. I could come meet you if you're close."

"What are you doing at One Hundred and Sixteenth Street?" I asked, curious.

"I had my interview at Columbia today." He sounded excited. "They're really thrilled about my research. I might even get a grant."

"Wow." I knew a hint of jealousy was in my voice. That could have been me, going to Columbia, teaching freshmen about the past, instead of writing articles about movies that got trolled by fans of actors who hated other actors.

"Who would have thought it, right? But I don't want to get too excited. It's not a sure thing. As the French say, don't count your chickens before they hatch."

"The French say that?" I giggled, feeling lighthearted for the first time in a week.

"Not in front of me, but who knows what they say behind closed doors."

"Oh, Blake, you always make me laugh." I giggled again and started walking toward the closest entrance. "I'm coming out of the park. I'll call you back with the cross street."

"Great."

After a few minutes I called Blake and said, "I'm at Ninety-Sixth Street."

"That's going to take me a bit." He laughed. "But I'm on my way. I'm coming down Amsterdam and then will cross over."

"I'll met you halfway." I headed out of the park, suddenly excited to see my old friend. Yes, things had ended awkwardly, but we'd always had a good relationship before that. I needed to speak to someone with no knowledge of everything that had been going on, someone who could offer me advice from a completely unbiased point of view—and I knew that person was Blake.

~

"So that's about it, then." I looked at Blake's face to see if he thought I was crazy yet. "I don't know who to trust or why any of this is happening or what to think, and I'm driving myself crazy."

"You really like him, don't you?" Blake's brown eyes were warm and supportive as he sat across from me in Tom's, the diner we loved to frequent on Broadway because the facade outside had been used in *Seinfeld*.

"What?" I sipped my coffee, perplexed at his question. "Like who? And that's your response after everything I just told you? That's the most important question after I just told you I was kidnapped?"

"It's important, yes." He nodded. "Not that your being kidnapped isn't important, but I've never seen you like someone before."

"Oh." I blushed and looked down. Maybe this had been a mistake. Maybe he still wasn't over me.

"I'm sorry." He leaned over and touched my hand. "I shouldn't have mentioned that."

"It's fine." I sighed. "I didn't expect you to believe me anyway."

"Oh, I believe every word you said." He suddenly looked serious. "We need to find Larry or Steve."

"We?" I looked up at him in surprise.

"I'm going to help you." He grinned. "I'm a regular detective, you know. I don't just piece together clues of the past. I piece together pieces of the future as well."

"You're a goof." I grinned. "A goof I've missed. And to answer your earlier question, yes, I really like him."

"Be still my beating heart." He clutched his chest and made a face. "For once I saw your face, I knew you were destined for another. My heart was slow to catch up and now it's hiding for cover."

"Blake." I rolled my eyes. "Did you pick up poetry as a side job in France?"

"No, but I did meet a nice French mademoiselle who taught me that to love and lose is the best experience one can go through in life."

"Oh?" I frowned.

"She was dramatic." He grinned. "She made my boring life more dramatic. She brought color and pain and poetry to my paltry life, and I'm grateful to her for it."

"I'm glad you had that experience."

"I guess we all have to grow up at some point." He cocked his head and smiled. "So when do we go back to Long Island to visit Mrs. Renee?"

"What?"

"She seems like the best link to everything, right?"

"After that call, I'm not sure she wants to see me again."

"Who cares what she wants?" He shrugged. "You want answers, right? Answers don't wait for convenient times."

"I guess." Beep beep. I grabbed my phone and saw a text from Jakob.

*Where are you?*

*What do you want?*

*To see you. To kiss you.*

I put my phone facedown on the table and turned back to Blake. "Sorry about that."

"Let me guess, that was Jakob, also known as Mattias Bradley?"

"You do catch on quickly." I nodded my head admiringly. "How did you know?"

"You looked happy when you looked at the screen." He licked his lips. "So obviously that means you like him, but don't want to like him."

"How can I like him in these circumstances?" I sighed. "Rosie thinks I'm crazy."

"Eh." He made a face, and I knew what he was thinking: *Don't listen to that jealous bitch.* Blake had never cared for Rosie.

"She thinks that I should trust David more than Jakob and see if I can talk to him to get some more answers."

"And what do you think?" Blake leaned back, his serious face set off by his tight, black curls. I stared at him, handsome and nerdy, and wondered why I'd never given him a chance romantically. He was the sort of guy I should have been with. I would feel safe with him. The problem was, I'd never had that chemistry with Blake.

"I think David is less trustworthy than Jakob." I made a face. "Though, I don't really know why."

"That's the problem. We don't have many concrete facts, do we?" Blake pulled out a pen and paper from his notepad. "Let's note down the facts that we do have."

"Primary research." I grinned.

"Nothing better, right?" He wrote *facts* in bold letters at the top of the page. "We know for a fact that your father died. We know for a fact that he used to work at Bradley Inc., we know for a fact that your mother died in a car crash, we don't know if that was an accident or not, we know that there were people that benefited from your mother's death, but we do not have an exhaustive list of those people."

"Well, we know Jeremiah Bradley was the number one beneficiary," I burst out.

"No, we don't know that for a fact." He shook his head. "Distance your emotions from the facts, Bianca. Don't forget you're a historian first."

"This is my family, Blake."

He gave me a sympathetic glance and continued, "We know for a fact that David and Jakob are brothers. We know for a fact that Larry Renee was your father's lawyer and also a lawyer for Bradley Inc. We know for a fact that you were kidnapped. We know for a fact that a third man, named Steve, was on the island with you and Jakob. We know for a fact that Steve and Larry have disappeared. What else do we know for a fact?"

"We know that Jakob is Mattias. And we know that he kidnapped me for revenge, and we know that he wanted to stop me from preventing the merger from going through."

"Actually, no. Emotions don't make good facts. And neither do assumptions. There is no substantiated proof that makes any of these things fact."

"What do you mean?" I frowned. "He all but told me that he kidnapped me for revenge."

"Yes, and he also told you that he and David were in on it together, yet they both seem to hate each other. And then there is the matter of Steve. What happened to him and why did he turn rogue? These are questions we must think about before we can even claim to know the answers as fact."

"You're not helping, Blake." I shook my head.

"Let's think of all the reasons why David and Jakob would want to kidnap you and then fall out."

"Maybe David got mad because Jakob released me earlier than he was supposed to."

"Perhaps." Blake nodded. "That would make sense on a very base level."

"Are you calling me stupid?"

"No." He grinned and leaned forward. "I'm saying that this is a much more complex subject."

Beep beep.

*Forget the kisses then. Can I see you?*

*No.*

*Please?*

*No.*

*Where are you?*

*Don't you already know?*

*No.*

*I'm with a friend. A male friend.* I knew as soon as I wrote the words that I was being catty, but I couldn't stop myself.

*I see. Good-bye.*

"Sorry about that. It was Jakob again."

"He really wants to see you." Blake looked thoughtful.

"He just wants to get some." My face reddened as I realized what I'd said. "Or maybe wants to tell me some more lies."

"Maybe he likes you as well." Blake scribbled something on his pad. "That could be a major clue."

"What could be a clue?"

"Maybe that's part of the reason he and David fell out. Maybe he strayed from the plan because he likes you."

"I doubt it very much." I made a face, but my stomach jumped in joy at the possibility. "I like him and I wish it was true and I can't stop thinking about him, but that's part of why I'm so paranoid about him."

"Don't beat yourself up. It's only natural to be confused. I'd be confused as well. When I went out with Astrid, I had no idea if I was coming or going."

"Astrid?" I smiled widely.

"Yes, Astrid."

"Unique name."

"Enough about me and Astrid, let's focus on you and your daytime-TV love triangle." He shook his head. "But first, let's go and get a locksmith for your door. And do me a favor—don't give anyone a copy."

"I'll give one to Rosie. We share keys in case we get locked out."

"For now, don't do that." He looked serious. "Rosie is a suspect."

"What?" My jaw dropped. "No way. Rosie is not a suspect."

"You can give her a key when we rule her out for sure."

"Blake, Rosie is not a suspect!"

"Everyone is a suspect right now, Bianca."

"You're not."

"Well, that's because you know you can trust me." He grinned and I smiled back at him weakly. How many people were going to tell me that I could trust them? Those words meant absolutely nothing to me.

"Yeah."

"Also, I have an idea."

"An idea?" I leaned forward. "What's that?"

"I'm going to see what I can find out about this elusive Steve."

"Oh?"

"He's the biggest clue we have right now." Blake nodded to himself. "I think if we figure out who this Steve is and what his motivations were, we can start to crack this code."

"Don't you think we should be focusing on the Bradleys? I feel like David and Jakob will have the biggest clues."

"I don't think so." He shook his head. "The most obvious suspects are usually the least likely culprits."

"Or the most likely."

"They are definitely involved, but I don't see either of them as being the kingpin or the don, so to speak."

"The don?" I sipped my coffee again. "Interesting you use that term. I met a guy recently who mentioned the Mafia to me."

"You think the Mafia is involved?" Blake's eyes lit up.

"No." I shook my head. "I sincerely doubt it."

"Yeah, me too. Kidnapping you and taking you to an exotic island is not their style. More like kidnapping and locking you in a black cellar with rats scuttling around your feet as the stench of rotting bodies nauseates you, while they whip you for information."

"Really, Blake?"

"Sorry." He made a face. "Hey, that's a good thing though, right?"

"What? That I'm not in a damp cellar with rats nibbling on my toes?"

"No, that we have another fact." He scribbled on his notepad. "Not kidnapped by the Mafia."

"Yeah, that's really helpful." I shook my head.

"I told you." He grabbed his pad and jumped up. "Let's go and take care of your lock, then I'm going to head to the library to do some research."

"Library?" I dropped a $5 note on the table.

"Yeah, I don't want anyone tracking my IP address. Who knows what sites I'm going to have to hack into to get information on Steve?"

"Blake, I don't want you to get into any trouble."

"It's no trouble." He looked around him. "This will be fun."

"I'm glad you think so." I made a face at him as we walked to the subway station.

"Hey." He grabbed my shoulders and stopped walking. "I don't think this is fun fun. It's scary as shit, but I don't want you to focus on that. Focusing on all the psychos in the world isn't going to help us solve this."

"I know." I reached over and hugged him. "I'm glad you called me. I don't think I could have asked for anyone better to help me."

"You're not going to start ignoring my calls again, are you?"

"I wasn't ignoring your calls," I lied.

He rubbed the top of my head. "It's okay, Bianca." He

whispered in my ear, "I'm the last person you need to be worried about right now."

"Go to the library now." I smiled at him widely, feeling positive and strong. "I'll be okay. I can deal with the lock. You go now and start researching."

"You sure?"

"Yes, I'm positive." I nodded. "I got this."

~

The letter was waiting on my doormat when I arrived home. It looked like the first letters I'd received. My heart didn't even skip a beat as I opened the envelope. I read the letter quickly, trying not to read too much into the words.

*It's time for you to know the truth. It's time for me to lay all my cards on the table. It's time for me to make you mine once and for all.*

*Mattias*

I walked into the apartment and went directly to my bedroom. I collapsed onto the bed, laying my head back on the pillows that had supported me and Jakob just a couple of days ago. So he had decided to come clean. I can't say that I was shocked, but I was surprised. Why had he decided that now he wanted to tell the truth? Did he think he owed it to me? Did he feel guilty that he had taken me once again? Did he feel my pain knowing that my parents weren't as squeaky-clean as I'd thought?

Or was he doing this because I told him I was with another man? I couldn't believe that I was playing games with him. Not when so much was going on, but I just couldn't stop myself from thinking about him. I was glad that Blake had contacted me. I wondered what he would find on Steve. I was annoyed that I hadn't thought to research Steve myself. I just wasn't thinking logically, but I knew that was due to the absolute confusion in my life. I'd tried to be light with Blake, but I was still pretty shattered about everything.

I wasn't sure what devastated me more: knowing that Jakob had betrayed my trust or knowing that my parents weren't who I'd thought they were. All those years, I'd believed that my father was a broken man because of my mother's death. I'd thought he was heartbroken because he'd lost her. Now I didn't know what to believe. I didn't want to believe that my father was responsible for my mother's death. I didn't want to believe that my mother had had an affair. However, I wanted to hear what Jakob had to say. I wanted to know why he'd lied about who he was. I wanted to know if what we had experienced together had been real in any way.

Then I remembered something my father had told me when I was a teenager with my first crush. What was it he'd said? "Be careful who you give your heart to, Bianca. You never know who will rip your heart out so completely that you'll never be able to get over it." At the time, I'd just put it down to his still being depressed by my mother's death, but now that I thought back to it, it could have had so many other meanings. Maybe she *had* cheated on him. Maybe my mother wasn't the saint I'd grown up thinking she was. Did she ruin Jakob's parents' relationship? Had she had another child? Did I have a sibling? If so, where was the person? And did that person know about me?

I shivered as I realized that someone who knew I was a relative could be walking around the city while I knew nothing. It saddened me to know that everything I thought about true and eternal love might be false. My poor dad! How he'd suffered. I tried to banish my thoughts of self-pity—they were useless to me. I needed to remember what Blake had said. I needed to think about everything objectively, without letting my emotions get the better of me. I couldn't look at Jakob as my lover or my enemy. I had to look at him as a man with an agenda. An agenda I needed to get to the bottom of.

Then a text came. *There will be a car waiting to pick you up outside your apartment at 8 pm. It will wait for 15 minutes. The choice is yours. Do you want to become mine once and for all?*

I dropped my phone on the bed, my heart pounding fast. What was I supposed to think? Rationally, I knew I'd be a fool to go. What was I expecting from Jakob? And what did he mean, *become his once and for all*? If I was honest with myself, I had become his the first time we'd made love. My body craved his touch the way my lungs craved air. I needed him to survive. I needed him to exist. Yet, I still had so many questions. Who was Jakob? Could I ever get used to calling him Mattias? Could I trust him?

~

I didn't consciously make the decision to go, but as I found myself in the shower, I knew I had no other option. I had to see this through to the bitter end. I was addicted to Jakob. I needed him to take me to the edge, even if that meant falling over and into the abyss. Stepping out of the shower, I dried my body slowly, thinking about what the night would bring me. I splashed some of my Gucci II perfume on my body and looked through my underwear drawer. What should I wear to make him think I was sexy, but hadn't come trying to look sexy? I opted for a matching black lace bra and panties. They were simple, but enticing. I shimmied into my favorite black skirt before pulling on a flowy, white blouse. I brushed my hair and blow-dried it before using a flatiron to straighten out all my waves. My hair was shiny and silky and bounced against my back softly as I applied my makeup almost as well as they had done in the department store a couple of months ago. I smiled nervously at my appearance, barely recognizing the girl in the mirror. She didn't look like Bianca London. The muted green-brown eyes shining back at me possessed a bravery and stubbornness I didn't feel. I glanced at the clock. It was minutes to eight. I had to make my way downstairs if I wanted to go through with the plan. I felt like a traitor to myself as my heels clicked down the steps. I was serving myself up on a platter to a man that had lied to me and been responsible for my abduction to a deserted island. I was a fool, plain and simple, but in that moment I just didn't care. All I could think about was him inside me, calling out my name, holding me close to him. All I could see was the look in his eyes as our two bodies became one melded together by a spark so pure that our passion seemed never ending.

My timing was perfect—a black limo pulled up as soon as I walked outside. The lady beggar across the street looked at me as I made my way toward the car. I knew she was wondering what was going on, if I was some sort of escort. It wasn't every day that a black limo pulled up outside my building, and I'd certainly never been in one before. A driver jumped out of the car before I could blink and made it to the pavement to open the door for me.

"Good evening, Ms. London."

"Hello." I waited for him to give me his name, but he didn't say anything else. "Are you taking me to see Jakob?" I asked him lightly as I slid into the back of the limo. "I mean, Mr. Bradley?"

"Mr. Bradley is waiting for you, Ms. London."

"He's not planning on taking me anywhere, is he?" I laughed nervously. "Like to another island?"

"Would Ms. London like to vacate the car?" the driver said, his expression never changing.

"Do you think I should?" I asked him softly, feeling uneasy. Why wasn't he even smiling at me?

"Mr. Bradley is waiting for you, Ms. London." I stared directly into his eyes. They were emotionless and it scared me.

"Do you call him Jakob or Mattias?" I asked softly.

Only then did I see a small crack in his mask. His eyes darkened and he looked at me with a stoic expression. "We all call him Mr. Bradley," he said softly. "We daren't call him anything else, unless he gives us permission."

"I see. Thank you."

He blinked once as I sat there in the car. "You'd still like to go?"

"Yes." I nodded. "Take me to Mr. Bradley." He closed the door without a word and I sat back, waiting to be driven to Jakob's house. I had no idea what it was going to look like. Would it be opulent, like his hotel? Or would it be more modest, like David's apartment? What did he have planned for me? What secrets was he going to divulge?

I reached into my handbag to text Rosie and let her know where I was going, but then I remembered I'd left my phone on my dresser. I bit my lower lip, annoyed that I had forgotten it. If anything happened, it was going to be hard for me to call someone for help. Though I wasn't sure whom I would call: Rosie or Blake? I was glad when I felt the paper-towel-wrapped knife still in my bag. If anything happened, I'd stab him hard. Thinking about stabbing Jakob took me back to the island and that final night with Steve. How confused I'd been. For a few seconds I hadn't known whom I could trust. It was ironic that after all that I hadn't been able to trust either of them.

"We're here, Ms. London." The car arrived at a gated entrance and we waited for the doors to open. "Are you sure you want to go inside?"

"I'm sure." I nodded. I needed answers. I needed to know what was going on. I needed to make sure that Larry was okay. His wife had left the diner in tears, and I hadn't known what to do or say. How could I apologize? I didn't even know what had happened to him. This was about more than just me now. Larry's comments had ignited the questions in my head. What was going on here? Why had he told me to not think about Mattias? What clues had Jakob been trying to give me earlier? I bit on my lower lip as I remembered the name he'd give me. Why had he mentioned Tyler Durden and *Fight Club*? Was Tyler Durden a clue related to my brother? Was that what he'd been trying to tell me. I wished that I had my phone on me so I could google it.

"Have you ever heard of Tyler Durden?" I asked the chauffeur as he held the door open for me.

"The guy from *Fight Club*?" He frowned. "The Brad Pitt character?" He stepped back as I got out of the car.

"Yeah, him." I tried to remember the plot of the movie, but my mind was coming up blank. Why was this the only movie I didn't know about? "He fights with the Edward Norton character, right?"

"I think so." The driver nodded. "They fight, but he doesn't really . . ." His voice trailed off as he closed the door. "I'm sorry, miss, but I must take you to a special room now. You must listen carefully and follow all instructions. Do you understand?"

"Yes." I took a deep breath. What was going to happen to me now? "What happened with Tyler? What didn't he really do?" I asked the man, but he didn't respond. I followed him into the house stiffly. It wasn't what I had expected. The Gothic-looking house, majestic and dark, didn't fit my image of Jakob. Though I supposed my image of Jakob was as false as everything else I thought I knew about him.

"Into the study, Ms. London." He opened the door for me. "You're to put on this blindfold and these earmuffs and then to come with me."

"A blindfold and earmuffs?" I frowned. "Why?"

"I just follow orders, ma'am."

"I guess." I sighed. "Is that it?"

"I'm to handcuff you." He looked down.

"Handcuff me?" I shivered in the cold room. "Is that necessary?"

"Yes, ma'am."

"Am I going to be able to leave?" My head was telling me to make a run for it. None of this was sounding like a good idea. None of it at all. But a part of me was excited. What did Jakob have planned? My nerves were on edge thinking about what he was going to do to me. Implicitly I trusted that he wouldn't harm me, at least not physically. He'd already had plenty of chances to harm me if he wanted to. He was playing a game with me—some sort of sexual game. And I knew that it was the only way to get answers out of him. I didn't know if I was capable of winning, though. The way my heart was beating told me that I was too emotionally involved to be smart. However, a part of me didn't care. A part of me was willing to accept whatever went down.

The man just stared at me without answering and I held my hands out to him. "Handcuff me then," I said bravely, swallowing hard. This might have been the stupidest move I'd made in my life, but I wasn't going to know unless I went along with it. The man picked up the handcuffs and locked them over my wrists before blindfolding me with a piece of dark silk. I couldn't see a thing through the material and I was already beginning to regret my decision.

Then he slipped a pair of earmuffs over my head and walked me slowly back out of the room and through the house. We walked for what must have been a little over a minute, then I felt him lift me up and place me on what seemed to be a bed. I tried to control my breathing as I felt my head hit the pillow. What did Jakob have planned for me?

I felt my earmuffs lifted up and then lips pressed against my ear. "In *Fight Club*, Edward Norton's character was fighting Brad Pitt's character, Tyler Durden, but you find out at the end of the movie that he was fighting himself," the voice whispered quickly in my ear before replacing the earmuff. I lay there, my head spinning as I tried to comprehend what he was saying. Then I remembered. Edward Norton was really fighting himself. Tyler Durden didn't really exist.

I lay back for a few minutes thinking, then I felt the soft touch of fingers on my leg. I was no longer alone. The fingers ran up my leg in a familiar way, tickling and teasing me at the same time. I stilled as he ran his fingertips all the way from my ankles and up my thighs, pushing my skirt up as he touched me. He grabbed my wrists and I felt him taking the handcuffs off. I sighed in relief that I was no longer constrained, but then froze as I felt a piece of rope replacing the cuffs and tying my wrists together. Why was he putting rope on my hands?

His fingers ran over my stomach and then across my breasts. I was ashamed that my nipples were already hard, but he seemed to enjoy that, as he ran his palms across them several times. I lay there, unsure of what to think and feel. My body was on fire and my mind was in shock. Then he slipped the earmuffs off. My ears adjusted to the sound in the room—all I could hear was his heavy breathing and the sound of my own heartbeat. I wanted to say something, but my voice wouldn't work.

"You look so beautiful." The voice was deep and muffled and I didn't understand why it was so hard to hear him. He leaned down and I felt his lips pressed against mine, kissing me softly. I lay there passively, something in me not feeling right about the situation. I turned my face to the side and he groaned, grabbing it roughly.

"Don't turn away from me, Bianca," he muttered, and kissed me again, his fingers slipping down my stomach. "Did you think I'd just let you go? Did you think I'd let you play me and not do anything?" He rubbed the outside of my panties roughly. "I've wanted you for so long now." I breathed in his musky scent, and while it was familiar, I knew it wasn't Jakob. It wasn't my Jakob at all.

I felt him sliding my panties down and felt my legs being pushed apart and fingers touching me before he kissed me again. I breathed in his fragrance one more time and I finally understood the reference to Tyler Durden. It didn't make sense, but it was the only logical answer. Jakob wasn't Mattias. There was no Mattias.

"Jakob?" I whispered, and the man next to me froze, telling me all I needed to know. "I know who you are. I know what's going on." My voice was angry.

"You do?" His voice sounded hard and I marveled at what a good actor he'd been. Only a few times had I ever seen him so upset. He'd played me well, though I'd thought I was playing him. He kissed me hard again, then squeezed my breasts. I felt his tongue between my legs and my body buckled as I closed my thighs on his face and tried to shift away from him. The feel of his tongue and his technique confirmed it to me. I wasn't sure why I'd been so stupid. All along I should have known the truth. When I was on the island, Jakob had made it clear to me that his father had never married his mother. He wasn't David's full brother. David's mother was married to Bradley senior, David's mother was Bradley senior's wife. And Jeremiah Bradley would never have given his bastard the power over the company that Mattias wielded. That meant that Jakob was not Mattias. And if everything I was starting to think was true, it also meant that a far greater lie had been taking place for a long time.

"Do you like this, Bianca?" His mouth left my wetness and he kissed me on the lips. I felt his hands on my face as he slid the blindfold off. "I want you to watch me as we make love." He grinned down at me, his green eyes lacking emotion. "This will be our first time." He touched my face lightly. "I want it to be perfect for you, Bianca."

I blinked up at David, not feeling surprised. I'd known from the minute he'd touched me that it wasn't Jakob. I stared into his eyes and he gave me a small half smile. Now I knew why Jakob had told me not to trust David. He had been up to no good from the very beginning.

# nine

"What are you doing, David?" I blinked up at him, my body still shaking slightly from the tingles and anger that were invading my body in equal waves. I tried to kick him and he laughed, a hollow, unsympathetic sound as he held me down.

"What you wanted me to do." He grinned at me and ran his fingers across my lips. "What you've been wanting from the beginning."

"Where's Jakob or Mattias?" I asked softly, though part of me already knew the answer. It was the only answer that made sense, though it didn't make any sense. The driver had known that it was a setup and he'd tried to warn me as best as he could, but I'd been stupid. I wanted to kick myself at how many stupid decisions I'd made.

"Mattias couldn't be bothered to come. He told me to take care of you for him." David shrugged and his right hand stroked up and down my stomach. His fingers felt rough and aggressive and I shifted on the bed uncomfortably.

“David,” I pleaded. “Please untie me. Don’t do this.”

“Why? You going to be a fucking tease again?” He stared down at me, nostrils flaring. “You think you can just be a cocktease and get away with it?”

“David.” I took a deep breath. “Please, don’t do this. This isn’t who you are. This isn’t who we were.”

“You think you can play me? You think that after everything you can just use me and expect that you’re not going to pay?”

“David . . .” I froze as I heard a loud bang. “What’s that noise?” I frowned as he jumped up as well.

“Who’s there?” he shouted, and walked toward the door. I struggled, attempting to free my bound hands as he walked away.

“What the fuck is going on?” Jakob burst into the bedroom, his eyes manic as he stared at David and then at me tied to the bedpost. “Bianca.” Jakob’s eyes narrowed as he stared at my panties around my ankles and my wrists tied above my head. “What did he do to you?” Jakob’s voice was hoarse and he looked like Mars, the god of war, angry and ready to go to battle.

“Please untie me,” I begged him. He strode toward me as if carried under a power not his own.

“Mattias to the rescue.” David laughed bitterly.

Jakob quickly untied my wrists, his face angrier than I’d ever seen it before. He glanced into my eyes and stroked the hair off my forehead. “You okay?” he whispered down at me, and I nodded. “Good.” He touched my cheek and turned around.

“She looks pretty tonight, doesn’t she?” David laughed.

“Shut up before I kill you, you motherfucker.” Jakob turned toward David. “I will fucking kill you.”

“Why?” David sneered. “I had her before you. And she didn’t say no as I just brought her to orgasm again. She loves my tongue, though I think she’d love my hard cock even better. She used to love it when I . . .” He started laughing maniacally.

I stared at him in shock as he laughed. Jakob walked over to him and punched him in the face.

I watched as David fell back and looked at his brother with hatred. “What the fuck?” David glared at Jakob. “Bros before hos, man.”

“I don’t know what you’re playing at, David.” Jakob pulled him up off the floor. “I could kill you right now without blinking an eyelid.”

“You’re just jealous of me. You always were and you always will be,” David sneered. “You’re the illegitimate son. You’ve always had something to prove. You can’t stand being under me. You can’t stand that I run the company.”

“What are you talking about?” I looked at both of them in confusion. What was going on here? “I thought you didn’t work at Bradley.” I looked at David in confusion. “I thought you just lived off of your trust.”

“Stupid girl,” he sneered. “You still don’t get it? I’m the

one in charge. The big boss. The CEO. I more than work at Bradley Inc., I run it." He smirked as he watched me.

"But Mattias . . ." I didn't even know why I was bringing him up anymore. I didn't understand what the fuck was going on, but I knew that there was no Mattias.

"There is no Mattias," Jakob said softly, confirming what had been in the back of my mind for a little while. He turned to look at me, a look of pity on his face. "There is no Mattias, Bianca."

"I don't understand." My voice cracked. "What do you mean? Why would you create a fake person?" David started laughing, a loud, hysterical sound. I stared at his face and noticed just how calculating he looked, just how deceptive his eyes were. How had I ever thought this man was boyish and charming?

"Did you really think you were that smart, you dumb bitch? Did you really think I would lead you to Mattias?" David looked at me disdainfully. "Did you really think you could con your way into a shareholders' meeting of one of the biggest companies in the world and not be found out?"

I chewed on my lower lip and stared at him, not saying anything.

"Larry called me and told me that you'd asked him to procure shares to come to the meeting. We both knew that there was only one reason for you to be at that meeting."

"Larry told you I was coming?"

"Yes, 'Uncle Larry' told me everything." David laughed.

"He told me about the boxes of papers your dad left for you. I told him to destroy them, but I think he felt guilty, so he handed them to you. Worst decision he ever made. If he'd just destroyed those boxes, he could have saved all of us a lot of aggravation."

"You knew this?" I looked at Jakob with hurt eyes, but he didn't respond. "So there is no Mattias?" I looked at David. "So all this time, all those days you said you were asking him to join us for dinner, you were lying."

"What do you think?" David sneered. "Didn't you ever think it was weird that there were no photos of Mattias and no one had ever met him and that he didn't even go to his own company's shareholder meeting?"

"I just don't understand. It says he's the CEO on the company website. Your father's bio says he has two sons, Mattias and David Bradley."

"I did have a brother." David shrugged. "He died when he was a baby, but his name wasn't Mattias. Mattias was a name that Larry came up with, actually." David laughed.

"Larry?" I frowned. "Larry *knew* there was no Mattias?"

"I should think so. He's the one who did all the legal paperwork for the corporation. He's the one who took care of everything."

"Why?"

"My father thought it would be easier on me if people thought there was someone else in charge of the corporation." David looked cynical. "And it's true. People don't bother me as much. I don't have gold diggers and other leeches chasing me down so much. People think I'm the playboy son, nothing important—and that's how I like it."

"You *knew*?" I turned to Jakob. "You knew there was no Mattias and you didn't tell me?"

"What could I say?" He pursed his lips, his blue eyes unreadable as he stared at me.

"I don't even know what to say." I shook my head, my entire body shaking from the shock. "You deliberately let me believe you were Mattias."

"You're the one who assumed I was Mattias. I never said I was." He shook his head and walked toward me. "You asked me if I was David's brother and I said yes. I never said my name was Mattias. I never lied to you, Bianca. I tried to tell you that there were things you didn't know."

"Don't be mad at him," David cut Jakob off. "You can't believe that a stupid little girl like you can manipulate us? We're Bradleys, Bianca. You can't just show up and act like Nancy Drew and not set off our warning signals."

"Is that why you both threatened Larry?" I looked back and forth at them. "Is that why he's in hiding? Did he set off your warning bells as well? Were you scared he was going to come clean about everything? And what did you do to Steve? Was that all part of the act as well? Where is he now? Laughing in some hotel room and counting all of the money you paid him?"

"What?" David frowned, his expression changing, and he

looked at Jakob. "What's she talking about? What threats did you send to Larry?"

"I didn't send anything to Larry." Jakob blinked and scratched his forehead, his expression changing.

"Larry was on our side." David frowned. "Larry's the one behind all of the paperwork. If there's anyone who wouldn't want any information to be revealed, it's Larry. I'd have no reason to threaten him."

"What about Steve?" Jakob stepped toward his brother. "Why did you tell Steve to go rogue?"

"What are you talking about?" David frowned. "I didn't even know Steve was going until after you both left. I didn't tell him to go rogue."

"It was your idea for me to kidnap Bianca and take her to the island. You're the one who told me that she was a gold digger like her mother and that she was trying to use you to get her hands on the Bradley money!"

"I just wanted you to warn her away. Give her a little scare." David pursed his lips. "I didn't tell Steve to do anything."

"Who were you speaking to?" I looked at David and poked him in the chest hard. "The last time I saw you before I caught you fucking that whore, who were you on the phone with?"

"What?" He frowned.

"When you were talking about me on the phone with someone, you said that something was too dangerous, but they could go ahead. Who were you talking to? I always thought it was Mattias. Was it Jakob, then? Or was it Larry? Is that why Larry's disappeared? Is he scared of you?"

"I don't know what you're talking about, Bianca." David shook his head. "I don't remember that conversation. There were many times I pretended to be talking to Mattias because I wanted you to believe that he existed. And I'm telling you once again, I don't know what's happened to Larry."

I looked into David's eyes and could see he was just as confused as I was. He wasn't the one who had been threatening Larry. But if not him and not Jakob, then who?

"Why did you send me those letters?" I asked softly. "And why did you leave us letters on the island as well? What did they mean?"

"What letters?" David frowned, and I could tell he didn't know about them either.

"Jakob?" I turned to him. "Are you the one who left the letters?"

"No." He clenched his fists. "It wasn't you and Steve?" He grabbed David's shirt tight.

"No," David squeaked out. "I didn't send any letters and I didn't send Steve to the island and tell him to listen to me, instead of whatever he had planned with you. I just wanted to scare you, Bianca. I just wanted you to back off. Jakob was taking care of that for me. I don't know anything else."

"What do you know about my mother's death? What do you know about my father's share in the company? Why did you want me to back off?"

"I didn't know anything. Larry contacted me and said we might have a problem. He told me he gave you some boxes from your father and then you asked him to get you shares so you could attend the shareholders' meeting. He warned me that we needed to be careful. Larry is the one that had the most to lose. He's the one that set everything up."

"So what the fuck has happened to Larry?" Jakob said in an annoyed tone, and we all just looked at each other, our faces a mix of anger, hatred, suspicion, and worry. I felt as if I'd uncovered a huge secret, but it wasn't satisfying. All it had done was expose a deeper and scarier void of unknown. We'd all thought that we were the main players in this game, but we were all just puppets. Someone else was pulling the strings, and none of us knew who or why.

# ten

Jakob and I left David's house in silence. I sat in the passenger seat and stared out the window as he drove me home, the tension thick in the air. I could hear my own heart beating as I sat there tensely listening to Jakob's fingers tapping against the steering wheel.

"You're not going to say anything?" he said finally, and I could feel his eyes on me.

"What am I supposed to say?"

"Maybe you could tell me why you let David put his—"

"Are you fucking kidding me?" I turned to Jakob angrily. "Did it look like I *let* David do anything?"

"Did you tell him no?"

"Not at first," I acknowledged. "I thought it was you."

"How could you—"

"I was blindfolded, Jakob, and the letter was from Mattias. I thought it was just some kinky shit you were into."

"Did you like it?" he growled.

"Did I like what?" My voice rose.

"When he touched you."

"I'm not talking about this." I shook my head. "You're a fucking asshole to even be asking me this shit. What do you think? I was taken advantage of, Jakob."

"But it's not the first time that he—"

"Enough, I'm not talking about this. I'm not going to let you make me feel bad for something where I was the victim."

"I'm sorry." He banged his fists against the steering wheel. "I should have gotten there quicker."

"It's not your fault." I sighed. "How did you know I was even there?"

"The driver called me."

"What?"

"He thought I should know. He had a bad feeling about what was going on. He had a feeling David had fooled you."

"I see." I looked away, my face feeling warm and angry. "But he didn't tell me."

"His loyalty isn't to you."

"Obviously not."

"I'm sorry he did that to you. It kills me to know what he did to you."

"It kills you for yourself or it kills you for me?"

"I'm just a man, Bianca. I don't purport to be perfect. I don't purport to be unselfish. I'll admit that I'm jealous. I'll admit that I don't want another man touching you. And I don't want you to be in that position again."

"What are you doing?" I frowned as Jakob drove past my apartment building. "You just passed my building."

"I know that."

"I know you know that, stalker." I glared at him. "Tell me *why* you drove past it. I want to go home."

"I'm looking for a parking space."

"Parking space?" My jaw dropped. "Why? You don't think I'm going to invite you in, do you?"

"Bianca, we're not done talking."

"I'm done talking to you."

"Bianca, we need to talk. Stop being so obstinate."

"I'm not being obstinate just because I'm saying you're not coming into my apartment. There is no way I'm going to let you come in and tell me more lies."

"I was trying to keep you safe!"

"Safe with lies. Ha." I laughed bitterly. "Sure you were, and you did a great job. A really great job."

"I'm sorry I was a jerk." He pulled over and turned toward me. "I'm sorry."

"You can't park here." I shook my head and looked out the window. "If a cop sees you, you're going to get a ticket."

"I don't care about getting a ticket." He sighed. "I can't get you out of my fucking mind."

"And that's my fault?"

"I'm not saying it's your fault. I'm just saying this is confusing." Jumping out of the car, he hurried over to my side and opened the door.

"What are you doing?" I glared at him. "I told you that you can't park here."

"I don't give a shit. Get out." He leaned forward and unbuckled my seat belt. "Get out!"

"You're so bossy."

"I think that's what you like." He smirked as his hand brushed my stomach. He stopped for a second and stared into my eyes. "You need a man to boss you around."

"Like hell I do."

"You didn't seem to mind when we were on the island."

"That's because you were providing water and food."

"And shelter."

"I wouldn't consider your body a shelter," I said smartly, and smiled sweetly.

"Oh, you wouldn't?" He licked his lips and leaned toward mine. "I definitely found your body to be a shelter. You kept my cock very warm every night."

I gasped, my face turning red with embarrassment and excitement. "You're a pig!"

"A pig that wants you to get out of the car." He grabbed my hand and pulled me out of the car. "Let's go."

"I don't want you in my apartment."

"I know you're mad at me, but there is more going on here than we both think." He sighed and slammed the car door shut. "We need to talk. We need to figure this shit out. I think there is more to this than my stupid brother."

I tried not to roll my eyes. Had he really *just* figured that out?

"Look, Steve has disappeared." He pursed his lips as we walked. "So that's two people now."

"Two?"

"You said Larry disappeared as well."

"Yeah, but I thought you or David had something to do with that."

"We didn't." He shook his head. "It was Larry who told David there might be a troublemaker trying to stir things up."

"I played right into his hands, didn't I?" I sighed, embarrassed. I thought I'd been so clever. I'd thought David had had no idea of my charade. Turns out he'd known from the beginning. At the end of the day, it had been David playing me.

"You definitely weren't Sherlock Holmes." Jakob sighed. "I'm sorry."

"So you knew all along?" Embarrassment filled me as I remembered how clever I thought I'd been. Apparently I had fooled no one but myself.

"I knew that you were the daughter of the people that had ruined my parents' life. That's what I'd been told from the moment I was old enough to understand that my mother was depressed and sad every day."

"I'm sorry." I bit my lower lip. "I don't even know what to say."

"You have to understand that my whole life has been about getting justice for my mother. For making her life, her pain, not be in vain. I've always wanted the people to pay for making her life a misery."

"But it wasn't really a misery, was it?" I said softly.

He stopped and frowned at me. "What do you mean?"

"She had you, right?" I gazed at his handsome and inscrutable face. His eyes were dark and heavy, and for a moment I could see the little boy in him. I could imagine him staring at his mother in confusion and sorrow, wondering why she was always sad. I could imagine the heartache of living with that every day and not being able to do anything about it.

"What do you mean, she had me?"

"She had a wonderful, handsome son. And she loved you, right?"

"She loved me because I was my father's son." He shrugged.

"No." I shook my head. "She loved you in spite of that. She did everything for you. I remember you told me that. She did everything to make sure you succeeded. She loved you more than life itself. You were her reason for living."

"I wasn't enough to keep her living, though."

"What do you mean?"

"It doesn't matter." He shook his head. "We have more pressing things to worry about."

"I wish you would let me in a bit more." I was sad that he wouldn't discuss his feelings with me. Yes, I hated him for lying to me and I hated him for being a part of this whole craziness, but a part of me was happy. I was happy that he wasn't this fictional evil character, Mattias. I was happy that our time on the island was real, at least in part. The feelings he had for me were genuine. I knew now that wasn't part of his act. It wasn't enough to make me forget everything that had happened, but he liked me. I shivered just thinking about how I felt when he touched me. I was so screwed.

"I've let you in more than anyone else in my life." His voice was soft. "I've trusted you with information and thoughts and feelings that I've never trusted anyone with. Even when I thought your parents were part of the problem. Even when I was fighting that urge."

"You really think my mother slept with your father?"

"I do." He nodded.

"And why would that make my father bad?"

"Your father was the one who convinced my father not to be with my mother, and then your mother slept with my dad. So, yeah, it hurt your father as well, but he got what was coming to him."

"It wasn't my mother in the photo you sent me, you know." I touched his shoulder softly. "My phone died so I couldn't text you back, but that wasn't her."

"Are you sure?" He frowned, his eyes narrowed. "I was told that it was your mother."

"Who told you that?"

"Larry." Jakob clenched his fists. "Then he lied."

"Why would he lie about that?" I rubbed my forehead. "He was good friends with my father. Why would he lie? It doesn't make sense."

"Oh, Bianca, how did we get to this place? The only thing I'm sure of right now is the burning passion I have for you. I crave you like a drug, Bianca. A drug I know is bad for me, but one I can't stop myself from wanting and needing." He gripped my shoulders and pulled me to him.

"We're a mess, aren't we?" I sighed and stared up into his eyes, feeling close to tears. "I feel numb, Jakob. A part of me feels so numb inside. I don't even know what to think or feel anymore."

"Let me be your warmth and strength, Bianca. Let me help to make you whole." He gripped my shoulders. "This is bigger than both of us. There are things we—"

"Jakob," I hissed at him, cutting him off. "Don't turn around yet, but I want you to look at the beggar lady across the street." I stared at her with her big Gucci sunglasses and old, shabby clothes. She was sitting almost directly across from us and she appeared to be staring in our direction. I studied her face as she smiled and thanked someone for giving her some money. My heart started racing as I saw the big, deep dimple in her right cheek. "Look at her face carefully," I hissed at him, my words coming out fast.

"What am I looking for?" He frowned and I shook my head and stepped back. He turned around slowly and looked at the lady. She was looking away from us now, but I knew what I'd seen.

"Let's go up to my apartment." I grabbed his hand. "Hurry." I ran toward the front door and got my keys out. "Come on."

"What was I supposed to have seen?" He sounded confused, but I ignored him as we entered the building.

"Hold on." I opened the door to my apartment and

raced into the living room, then ran to grab my cell phone. I opened my text messages and scrambled to show him the photo he'd sent me. I stared at it for a few seconds and my heart started racing even faster. "Look at this."

"What is it?" He grabbed my phone and looked down. "The photo of my dad and your mom?"

"That's not my mom." I was getting annoyed. "Are you slow? I just told you that. That isn't my mom in the photograph, Jakob." I took a deep breath to calm my irritation. "Look at the photo carefully."

"What am I looking at, Bianca?" He sounded exasperated.

"Look." I leaned forward and ran my fingers over the screen so I could enlarge the photo. "Look." I pointed to the dimple in the woman's right cheek.

"So she has a dimple, so what?"

"So does the lady in the street." I sighed. "Didn't you look? That woman in the photo is the same one who's been begging in the streets."

"You think so?" He frowned and then closed his eyes. "Let me think." He stood there for a few seconds as he pictured the woman he'd just seen. His eyes popped open and he stared at me, staggered. "It's the same lady."

"I always wondered about her." I ran to the window and looked down at the street. "She's been there, in that spot, for the last year or so, and I always had a weird feeling about her. She'd always quote Bible verses at me, and she never really looked like someone that should have been in the street. There was one time I saw her and I noticed that she had perfectly even, straight, white teeth. I always wondered how her teeth were so white when it was unlikely that she brushed them twice a day and who knows how often she went to the dentist. I barely go every few years and . . ." I shook my head in disgust. "I can't believe I didn't suspect her before."

"I mean, what would you have thought?" Jakob sat down on my couch. "What was there to think?"

"Why is someone that appears to have money begging in the streets?" I groaned. "I'm an idiot."

"Should we go down and see who she is?" he asked me softly.

"Yes, let's." I nodded.

"What if she's your mother?"

I rolled my eyes. "My mother is dead, Jakob. You need to get over this fixation you have about my mother and your father. Larry obviously lied. Why can't you just accept that? My mother didn't have an affair with your dad. The beggar in the street is not my mother. The lady in the photograph is not my mother. My mother's dead. I don't know that lady from Eve." I was about to pull him up from the couch when my phone rang. I saw Rosie's name and groaned.

"Don't answer it." He shook his head. "We don't have time right now."

"I'll tell her I'm going to call her back." I shook my head. "Hey, Rosie."

"Bianca, where are you? I've been calling you." She sounded frantic. "I was worried about you after our call. You never called me back."

"I met up with Blake."

"Blake, your history-nerd friend?"

"Yes, I told you the history department was calling me. We went and got a coffee."

"Did you change your locks? How are you feeling? Do you want to come over and stay with me?" She kept rambling and I quickly interrupted her flow of words.

"Rosie, can I call you back?" I sighed. "You won't even believe what I found out today."

Her voice rose. "What did you find out?"

"There is no Mattias Bradley!" Jakob frowned at me and shook his head. I turned around and ignored him. "David created him."

"What?" Rosie's voice dropped. "He what?"

"Let me call you back, I have to go downstairs. There's a lady following me."

"What?"

"There's a lady watching me."

"Watching you?" Rosie repeated slowly.

"It's a long story. I'm going downstairs to confront her now."

"How do you know she's watching you?"

"I . . ." I paused as Jakob's hand went across my mouth. I turned to him with a frown and his eyes were a deep, fiery midnight blue as he shook his head. "I'll tell you later." I sighed. "I'll call you later."

"Bianca, wait." Rosie sounded worried. "Shall I come over?"

"No, no. It's fine."

"Bianca, hurry up," Jakob hissed at me.

"Who's there with you?" Rosie's voice rose.

"What do you mean?"

"I just heard someone in the background."

"No, no." I lied. "Maybe the TV."

"Okay." She sounded doubtful.

"I'll call you, okay." I hung up quickly. "What are you playing at?" I frowned at Jakob.

"Don't give away all your secrets." He frowned. "You don't know who you can trust."

"I can trust Rosie. She's my best friend."

"Uh-huh." He walked to the window. "Well, there goes our biggest clue."

"What do you mean?"

"Your beggar lady just hailed a cab." He sighed. "And for some reason, I don't think she'll be back."

"Shit." I ran to the window and watched a yellow cab pulling away from the curb. The pavement directly in front of the apartment was now empty. The strange woman was gone. "Maybe she saw us watching her." I stared at his blank expression. "Maybe she realized I'd caught onto her."

"Yeah, maybe."

"Wait." I froze as I remembered something that Larry's wife had said. I put my fingers to my lips and grabbed Jakob's hand, leading him to my bedroom.

"Oh, is tonight my lucky night?" He grinned as he spied my bed. I rolled my eyes and guided him into the bathroom, closing the door behind us. I turned on both sinks and the shower.

"Get in," I whispered, and pointed to the shower.

"What?" He frowned as I stepped into the shower with all my clothes on.

"Get in." I eyed him and wiped the water away from my face as my hair and clothes started to weigh me down.

"Okay." He grinned and I watched as he peeled all of his clothes off. I couldn't keep my eyes off his body as he stood there naked in front of me and stepped into the shower.

"You didn't have to get naked." I licked my lips nervously.

"You don't look so comfortable with your clothes on." He grinned and leaned into me. "Why are you in a shower with your clothes on by the way? That's an odd way to try and seduce me."

"I'm not trying to seduce you," I hissed, and my body trembled as he pulled my black skirt down. "What are you doing?"

"Getting you more comfortable." He threw the skirt onto the floor and then grabbed my top. "Don't you feel better now?" he whispered in my ear as he pulled my top off.

"Jakob," I moaned as I felt his cock pressing against my stomach.

"Why are we in here, Bianca?"

"I think my apartment is bugged," I whispered in his ear. "I went to visit Larry's wife and she told me her house was bugged, and I figured if they bugged her place, maybe they also bugged my apartment, and maybe that's how that lady in the street knew to leave. Maybe she's working with the same people who are behind everything."

"Hmmm." He nibbled on my earlobe. "I suppose that makes sense."

"Jakob," I groaned as I felt him unclasping my bra. We were both now naked in the shower.

"Yes, Bianca." He growled as he hands clasped my butt cheeks and pulled me into him.

"What are you doing?" I moaned as he pushed me back into the wall, his fingers running up and down my back.

"What do you think?" His mouth found mine and he kissed me hard, his tongue entering my mouth at the same time that his hand ran in between my legs.

"I—oh!" I cried out as he slipped a finger inside me.

"You're wet." He laughed against my lips.

"We're in the shower." I moaned and bit down on his lower lip.

"So?" He growled and picked me up. "Wrap your legs around my waist." He growled and pushed me back harder. "Hold on to my shoulders so you don't slip," he commanded me, his eyes dark with desire.

"Jakob," I moaned as I wrapped my arms around his neck, my breasts pressed against his chest.

"Yes, my dear?" He kissed me again as he guided his cock inside me slowly.

"Ooh," I cried out as his hands moved my hips slightly and he filled me up.

"I've wanted to do this since I saw you today." He

grunted as he moved his hips back and forth urgently. "You're mine, Bianca."

"Jakob," I cried out as his cock slid in and out of me with ease. "Oh, Jakob." My fingernails dug into his skin and I tightened my legs around him.

"Fuck." He pulled out, his breath coming heavy. "Give me a second." He kissed me furiously.

"What happened?" I whimpered, needing to feel him inside me again.

"I'm close to coming already," he growled. "What do you do to me?"

"I don't know." I held his face in my hands. "What do you do to me?" I muttered, not believing how easily my heart was opening up to him again.

"Give me a second." He grabbed a bar of soap and I slid down off him. He ran the bar of soap all across my body, cleaning every inch of me and scrubbing my skin with his hands.

"You don't have to do that," I gasped as he continued to clean me.

"I don't want you to feel dirty." He looked into my eyes. "I don't want you to think I'm an asshole who—"

"Jakob." I shook my head, not wanting him to continue. "Don't."

"I'm sorry." He slipped the soap between my legs and ran it back and forth, his fingers running over my clit as he attempted to soap every single part of me. "I think I might be falling in—"

"Jakob." I shook my head and leaned forward and kissed him. "Not now."

"But I want to tell you what I'm—"

"Right now, all I want you to do is fuck me." I groaned as my body trembled with need. I'd been so close to coming earlier. "Please," I begged him as the soap made its way across my nipples.

"Your wish is my command." With a grin, he dropped the soap on the shower floor and pressed himself into me. The water cascaded down our bodies for a few seconds before he lifted me up again to enter me quickly.

"Ooh!" I screamed out as he pushed me back against the wall and slammed into me. "Jakob," I cried out as his cock moved with an urgency I'd never felt from him before.

"Come for me, Bianca," he shouted, his eyes never leaving mine. "Come for me, my sweet darling," he growled, then opened the shower curtain wide, soaking the floor.

"What are you doing?" I gasped as my body approached orgasm. I held on to him and sank my teeth into his shoulder as the first body-shaking orgasm hit me.

"If they want to listen, they might as well see too." He winked at me. "This is for the cameras if there are any." He growled as he thrust into me two more times and then exploded inside me, his body shuddering against mine. "I'm falling in love with you, Bianca London. I'm not going to let anything happen to you," he whispered into my ear. "Let me prove to you that I can be a friend as well as a foe. Though, I want to be so much more than a friend."

I kissed his shoulder, suddenly exhausted as my feet slid back down to the ground. His arms wrapped around me and his body felt hot against mine as we just stood there. All of a sudden the last words of my father's letter hit my mind. It had said, *All I ask is that you be careful of who you trust. Friends can be foes and foes can be friends.* Maybe he would have wanted me to trust Jakob. Maybe Jakob was my knight in shining armor. Maybe he could help me solve this puzzle. I felt him kiss the top of my head as his hands rubbed my back. I snuggled into him, feeling safe. I trusted him, I really did. I just wasn't sure why I couldn't get that dire feeling from my stomach. Something was still off—I could feel it in my soul, but I had no idea what it was.

# eleven

"Pack a suitcase with whatever you want for the next couple of days." Jakob dried me off with my big, white, fluffy towel.

"Huh?"

"We're not staying here." He encircled my body in the towel and pulled me toward him. "So I need you to pack up some of your stuff."

"You're right, *we're* not staying here. However, I am." I glared up at him.

"No, you're not." He spoke matter-of-factly, as if he could just tell me what to do.

"Yes, I am." I tried to pull away from him.

"No, you're not. It's not even up for discussion." He gave me a pointed look. "You're leaving. You can do it willingly on your own two feet or I can carry you."

"You're not carrying me anywhere."

"Me Tarzan, you Jane." He winked at me. "I can beat my chest as well, if that makes you happier."

"You're a Neanderthal," I growled at him. "You think you can just control me?"

"You weren't complaining just now." He licked his lips and winked. "You seemed to like it when I took control of you just now, when I pulled your legs up and—"

"I was there. I don't need a play-by-play." I blushed. "And that's not the point. The point is just because we have sex, it doesn't mean that I trust you, and it doesn't mean I'm just going to move in with you and—"

"Umm, move in with me?" He smirked. "Moving a bit fast, aren't you?" He took a step back. "I never said anything about moving in with me."

"I didn't mean move in with you like that." I looked into his eyes, feeling embarrassed. "Stop laughing at me."

"I'm not laughing at you," he said with a straight voice. "Does it sound like I'm laughing at you?"

"Your eyes are laughing at me." I glared at him.

"My eyes are laughing at you?" His irises positively jumped for joy.

"Jakob," I growled.

"Yes, Bianca?"

"You're an asshole."

"I think I've told you before that I've been called a lot worse."

"I think I can understand why."

"As much as I love bantering with you, Bianca, I'd much

rather you get dressed, pack some clothes and whatever other junk you want, so we can leave."

"I already told you that I'm not—"

"Stop." He grabbed me and leaned forward. "Your apartment is bugged. People are threatening you. People are spying on you. You are not safe here. Now, you can call me whatever you want. You can fight me. You can punch me. You can do whatever you want once we make it to my place. But right now, I need you to pack your stuff and come with me. I'm not going to take no for an answer." He paused and gazed at my shocked expression and gave me a small smile. "No answer, Bianca?"

"You think I'm . . ." I stopped as his eyes narrowed.

"You have five minutes and then I pick you up and carry you out of here. I don't care if you're naked."

"You can't carry me out," I muttered angrily. "You can't carry me down the street. I'm not a hundred pounds."

"I can bench-press three-fifty." He smirked at me. "Trust me. I could carry you for ten miles if I wanted to."

"Whatever." I flounced out of the bathroom and hurried to my closet. He wasn't going to just leave, and I had a bad feeling that he would carry me out in the street in my bath towel.

"You have five minutes." He pulled on his pants and shirt and watched me as I grabbed some pants and a top and pulled them on quickly. I looked in the closet for a small duffel bag and pulled some random clothes into it. "Where are you going?" He followed me as I left the bedroom.

"I need to get my father's papers." I looked back at him and grabbed the plastic bag full of documents. "I'm pretty sure there are clues in here that I didn't get the first time around."

"What clues?"

"If I already knew, I wouldn't need to go through the papers again," I huffed.

"Anything else you want to bring?"

"Are you going to follow me around the apartment as I pack?" I glared at him.

"Why so hostile, Bianca?" He grabbed my hand. "Do you need me to soften you up again?"

"You're a pig. Do you really think that sex is the answer to everything?"

"Not to everything, no." He grinned.

"Do you take anything seriously?"

"I take everything seriously." He frowned. "Don't you get it, Bianca? I'm not the enemy here."

"Your first interest is yourself, not me." I shook my head. "Your first interest is getting revenge for your mother."

"We have the same interests, Bianca. We both want to figure out who the lady spying on you was. If she had an affair with my dad, why is she spying on you? Where is Larry? What happened to Steve?"

"Do you think David has anything to do with it?" I licked my lips and shivered, still not quite believing how David had tricked me so cleverly.

"No." Jakob frowned. "I don't think he could have pulled this off without telling me."

"I just don't get it." I gasped, a memory hitting me. "I can remember phone calls he had with Mattias." I remembered the time in his apartment when I'd stormed out and come back without his noticing. He'd been on the phone with someone—he'd said Mattias's name. He'd been making plans with someone. Whom had he been talking to if there was no Mattias? It just didn't make sense. Unless David and Jakob were both lying to me . . .

Maybe there was a Mattias, a third man. It would make sense. Maybe Jakob's new devotion, his supposed "openness," was still a part of the plan. Were David and Jakob in on this together? Could Mattias be, not Tyler Durden, but Verbal Kint from *The Usual Suspects*? "The greatest trick the devil ever pulled was convincing the world he didn't exist."

"Remember, Bianca, David knew from the beginning who you were and what you were up to. He planned every single detail he was going to let slip. Every thing he said and did was cleverly masterminded."

"Were you the one on the phone with David that night?" I asked Jakob softly. "Were you the one telling him what to do? If you're saying that David couldn't have done all this other stuff by himself, how did he come up with everything by himself?"

"Bianca." Jakob frowned. "Let's talk when we get to my place."

"What don't I know, Jakob?"

"There are things we both don't know." He walked into the bedroom and grabbed my duffel bag. "Is there anything else you need?"

"Does Mattias Bradley exist, Jakob?" I walked over to him and grabbed his chin. He blinked down at me, his eyes revealing nothing. "Does Mattias Bradley exist, Jakob?"

"What are you talking about?" He frowned. "We already told you there is no Mattias Bradley."

"Who else is in on this?" I glared at him. "It still doesn't add up. Who is David working with?"

"That's what you and I are trying to figure out."

"David has to know." I glared at him. "Why didn't we question him? He has to know."

"David is being used as a pawn, Bianca."

"What?"

"David doesn't know what's going on." Jakob grabbed my shoulders and led me to the front door. "Just trust me. We need to leave."

"You know more than you're saying, don't you?"

"There is more." He nodded. "We can't talk about it here."

"Tell me."

"Not now, Bianca," he growled, and opened the door. "Let's go."

"I hate you!" I said, glaring daggers at him. "You just can't be honest, can you? Is everything a lie with you?"

"Bianca, I admit that David and I planned the kidnapping.

He wanted you out of town because he was worried you would try and claim a share in the company before the merger, and I wanted to figure out what you knew about our parents. I don't know exactly what I thought was going to happen. However, things didn't go as planned. Someone else wanted us to kidnap you. Someone else wanted you to be scared. And I'm not going to let you out of my sight until I know who that someone else is, do you understand me?"

"But you lied to me, Jakob." My throat felt itchy. "It's hard to trust you fully, knowing that. It's hard for me to take anything that you say at face value now."

"I didn't lie when I said I think I'm falling in love with you." He stroked my hair back gently. "I didn't lie then."

"My friend Blake, the guy I told you I was meeting, he's investigating Steve." I stared at Jakob's face to see his reaction. "He knows everything that's happened. He knows who you are."

"Is he more than a friend?" Jakob's eyes narrowed and a hint of jealousy was in his tone.

"No, not at all."

"Good." He smiled suddenly. "I don't mind if he helps, then."

"Really?" I was confused.

"I want to know what happened with Steve as badly as you do. If he can help us with more information, that's great. Especially if there is nothing romantic between you."

I rolled my eyes, secretly pleased that he was jealous.

"I believe you, but, of course, I'll have to come with you

when you meet him." Jakob's eyes narrowed. "So that I can hear the information he provides at the same time."

"Uh-huh."

"Don't uh-huh me." He kissed me softly.

"I'll uh-huh you if I want to." I kissed him back.

"So we're good?" He leaned back, his expression more serious as he examined my face. "We trust each other now? We're working together now?"

I stared back at him for a few minutes, neither of us talking, just observing. He grabbed my hands and held them in his. I could feel his pulse racing and the tension in his body. His shoulders were stiff and his eyes were alert as he waited for my answer.

I went with my gut. "I do trust you. Let's figure this out."

"We're starting afresh now." He stroked my cheek tenderly, a wide smile on his face. "We've got this."

"I sure hope so," I whispered to myself as we made our way down the stairs.

~

God must have been smiling on Jakob. For some reason, his car was still parked in the loading zone with no clamp or ticket. We got into the car in silence, the warm, fuzzy feeling of sex in the shower long gone.

"You're going to be silent all the way?" He glanced at me as he started his car.

"What do I have to say?" I shrugged. "I'm still taking everything in. You're the one who needs to start talking."

“You’re so stubborn.” He sighed. “Of all the women in the world . . .”

“Of all the women in the world what?” My voice rose.

“I got stuck with you.”

“You got *stuck* with me?” My jaw dropped. “Is that a fucking joke?”

“Did you just learn the F-bomb?” He glanced at me. “I didn’t mean stuck with you in a bad way. I was teasing you. We just had a nice moment, no need to ruin it.”

“Excuse me?” I looked at him again and hid a smile. Two could play this game.

“You’ve been saying *fuck* a lot.”

My jaw dropped. “Are you seriously on my case about my language?” *Don’t laugh, Bianca.*

“The profanity, yes.” He laughed. “There’s no need to swear so much.”

“Fuck, fuck, fuck, fuckity fuck fuck, fuck off, you fucked-up piece of shit!” I fake-shouted at him, then burst out laughing in hysterics. “You should have seen your face just now.” I giggled. “You looked so worried.”

“Feel better?” He glanced at me with an eyebrow raised.

“You think you’re so cool, don’t you?” I stared at his profile. I felt so lighthearted being with him in this moment. A small seed of hope had taken root in my heart after our conversation, and for the first time ever I felt completely confident and comfortable with him.

“*You* think I’m cool, don’t you?” He smiled at me and turned onto the freeway. “By the way, you haven’t responded.”

"Responded to what?"

"My declaration of love."

"What declaration of love?" I rolled my eyes, my heart beating fast. Was this really the time? I wanted to hear it, but I was scared to respond. I didn't want us to move too quickly. The circumstances of our meeting were so extraordinary—what if that was the sole basis for our heightened feelings?

"I've told you twice now." He sounded unsure of himself.

"You told me what?"

"That I love you."

"No, you didn't. You said that you think you're falling in love with me. That's not the same." I paused. "And that's stupid, anyway."

"Why is it stupid?" he said softly.

"You don't do love, and you kidnapped me." *I can't let myself believe that he loves me. Not yet.*

"Things change."

"Kidnapping someone doesn't change." I turned to him. "That happened and can't be changed." *Though I'm falling in love with you as well, but I'm too chicken to tell you.*

"I'm falling in love with you, Bianca," he said again gently. "That complicates things, I know, but it doesn't have to."

"What things?" I asked softly, my brain going fuzzy. Did he really love me? Was he telling the truth? Should I tell him that I felt the same way?

"How do you feel?" For the first time, he sounded unsure.

"Feel about what?"

It was his turn to snap. "Bianca."

"I don't know," I lied. I already knew that I was in love with him.

"I see." He reached over and turned the radio on. "You don't have to sleep in my bed if that's what you're worried about."

"I'm not worried about sleeping in your bed," I said softly.

"I don't want you to think that just because you're staying with me that you have to be in the same bed with me. You don't have to sleep with me or have sex or anything. That's not why I'm—"

"Oh, shut up." I sighed. "You know I like you, Jakob."

"You do?" His tone changed and he sounded so upbeat that I laughed.

"Yes, I do. I don't know if I trust you, but that's another story."

"You don't trust me?" He sounded disappointed.

"I've been fooled more than once before." I tried to explain to him that it wasn't personal. "Forgive me if I don't know who to trust right now."

"But you came with me."

"You didn't really give me much choice."

"You chose to come with me. I didn't make you."

"I know. I want us to work on this together, and maybe it's for the best that I stay with you. Way too many people have access to my apartment right now."

"We'll get to the bottom of this, Bianca. I promise."

"Can you promise that we'll get to the bottom of this and

I'll still trust you have told me everything you know?" I asked him quietly.

He gave me a guilty look before turning back to the traffic. After about a minute's silence he finally answered simply, "No. I can't promise that."

"Jakob." The disappointment in my voice was evident.

"You don't know everything I know yet, but you will, I promise. I'm going to tell you everything I know, Bianca, and we're going to figure this all out together."

~

We pulled up outside a building and an elderly doorman rushed to the car door.

"Good evening, Mr. Bradley."

"Good evening, George." Jakob jumped out of the car, and before I knew it, he was grabbing my bag from the back while George opened my car door. He looked surprised when he saw me emerge from the car.

"Thank you, George," I said quietly.

"You're welcome, madam." He gave me a weak smile, his eyes never leaving my face.

"Are you okay?" I asked kindly, and that seemed to make him regain his composure.

"Yes." He rubbed his eyes and looked away. "Anything else you need, Mr. Bradley?"

"No, thank you, George." Jakob handed him something and George nodded his thanks. "This is Bianca, George. She'll be staying with me."

"Okay." George turned to me and smiled. "Welcome, Bianca."

"Thank you." I wished I had time to talk to him. Why had he looked at me as if he'd seen a ghost?

"If there is anything you need, please just ask, Ms. London."

"Thank you." Jakob and I were about to go inside when I froze, grabbing Jakob's arm. "Wait." I turned around and hurried back to George. "Wait, George!"

"Yes, Bianca?" He looked nervous.

"Why did you just call me Ms. London?"

"Isn't that your name?" he said weakly. "Isn't that what Mr. Bradley just said?"

"No." Jakob's voice behind me was deadly. "I said *Bianca*." He took a step forward. "How did you know her last name was London, George?"

"Oh, sir . . ." His face went white.

"Who have you been talking to, George?"

"No one, sir." He looked scared.

"Who's been around here, George?" Jakob's voice sounded deadly.

"No one, sir, I swear."

"How did you know she was Bianca London?"

My heart was pounding as I gazed at the two men. The tension in the air was electric. I was scared that Jakob was going to hit the old man, but I too was curious. How did he know my name?

"She looks like her mother, sir," he whispered. "As soon as I saw her, I recognized her."

"You knew my mother?" I gasped as I stepped forward.

"No." He shook his head. "I didn't know her. Not well. She only came twice."

"She came here twice?" I looked up at the expensive building in front of me. Why would my mother come here?

"What did she come for, George?" Jakob's voice was soft this time, though no less threatening.

"She came to visit your mother, Jakob." George's voice was low.

"They were friends?" I asked, surprised, and looked at Jakob, but he looked as shocked as I felt.

"No." George shook his head sharply. "Those two women were not friends."

"Oh." I wrapped my arms around my body, my heart sinking.

"Why did she visit my mother, George?" Jakob's voice was slow and deliberate. "What did she want?"

"I don't know exactly." George looked nervous. "I don't like to pry. I don't want to be in anyone's business. It's the only way you can be in a job like this for as long as I have been."

"You didn't hear anything?" I leaned forward, my face cold. "Nothing at all?"

"Well, the first time she came, I remember them screaming and shouting right in front of the building." He looked nervous. "I wasn't eavesdropping, but I couldn't help but hear them. And then she came back a second time. I remember it clear as day because I was so shocked when she came back. I didn't understand why she would return after the first time was so bad."

"What were they screaming?" I asked gently.

"All I remember hearing was 'He's mine.' " George stared at both of us.

"And what else?" Jakob said softly.

"I heard someone say, 'I'll kill you.' "

"What?" My jaw dropped. "Who said that?"

"I don't know." George looked apologetic. "I'm sorry. I don't know who said what." He gazed into my eyes. "I saw your face and it was like seeing into the past. You look just like her. So sweet, so innocent." He bowed his head. "I'm sorry if I've upset you, miss."

"No, it's fine." I looked at Jakob. His eyes were somber. I felt ashamed of myself. Maybe he'd been right all along. Maybe my mother *had* been having an affair with Jeremiah Bradley. Maybe my mother had ruined his mother's life after all. What did I really know about her? About anything? My heart dropped as I realized that maybe I wasn't representing the side of good after all.

~

"Welcome home. Well, to my apartment." Jakob opened his arms wide as we walked out of the private elevator and into his penthouse apartment.

"It's big." I laughed at my completely obvious comment. I stared around at the floor-to-ceiling windows and gazed out at the city lights. "What a view."

"What a view indeed." He turned to me. "Gorgeous."

"I'm talking about outside the window."

"I'm talking about you." He stepped toward me.

"So you were right," I said, unable to keep the sadness out of my voice. "My mom slept with your dad."

"We don't know what happened." He shook his head.

"I'm pretty sure we do."

"I don't blame you. My dad was a pig. He was obviously sleeping with a lot of women."

"Including my mom." I sighed. "I wonder if my dad knew."

"That would have been devastating for him." Jakob took my hand and pulled me to the couch with him. "Are you okay?"

"Not really." I closed my eyes. "The sky is closing in on me and I don't even know which side is up anymore."

"You're okay, Chicken Little." He rubbed my knee.

"How can you be so calm?" I glanced at him. "We basically just got confirmation that there was something going on with my mom and your dad."

"We confirmed nothing." He shook his head and paused. "Look at me, Bianca. All we've confirmed is that this whole thing is a lot more complicated than we both originally thought."

"What are we going to do?" I suddenly felt really glad to be with Jakob.

Then I heard the beep beep of my phone receiving a text. "I have a message." I pulled my phone out and frowned at the screen. "Actually, it's a voice mail." I frowned. "My phone didn't even ring, though."

"Listen to it." He nodded at the phone.

"Okay." I listened to the message and frowned. "Listen."

I put the phone on speaker and pressed REPEAT. "Bianca, it's Larry. I'm so sorry for everything. So, so sorry. Listen to me carefully. Look at the letters and the clues. The clues have the answers. Death wasn't the end, but the beginning." Then, after a scuffling noise, the message went dead.

"What was that?" Jakob frowned and rubbed his temple.

"I have no idea." I shook my head. "I hope he's okay," I said softly. "Even if he was a dirtbag."

"Hold on a second." Jakob grabbed my hands. "Remember the note you received on the island?" He frowned. "Didn't it say something about death?"

"Oh my God, it did!" I nodded, trying to think. "Hold on, let me think." I closed my eyes tightly and tried to remember what it said. "It said, 'Your life may be saved in death,' " I said after about a minute. " 'Your life may be saved in death.' "

"Doesn't that strike you as peculiar?" Jakob asked thoughtfully. "That the letter and Larry gave you such similar messages?"

"Definitely too similar to be coincidental." I nodded, my brain hurting. "I don't understand what it means."

"Let's think about it." Jakob stared at me for a second. "I think we've been looking at the clues incorrectly."

"What do you mean?"

"No." He shook his head. "I think we've been reading the notes as personal clues, as if the meanings were intended for us—but what if the clues are more general? What if the clues have nothing to do with us? What if the clues are pointing to someone else altogether?"

"Someone else?"

"Someone else, something else." He shrugged. "Just not us."

"I never thought of that." I bit my lower lip and tried to remember the other clues and notes. "Get me a pen and paper, please. I want to try and write down all the clues I remember."

"Okay." He jumped up and ran into another room and then returned with a pen, notepad, and small box.

I frowned as I looked at the small box. "What's that?"

"Remember I told you that you didn't know everything?" He sat next to me. "I was getting notes as well."

"What?" My eyes widened. "What?"

"I'm sorry I didn't tell you." He sighed. "I didn't want to mention it before because I didn't want to overwhelm you, and I wasn't really sure if there was any connection before."

"I see." I looked away, feeling hurt, but not wanting to argue, not now. Not when we needed to put our minds together and try to work this all out. I grabbed the pen from his hand and scribbled down all the clues I could remember.

The first note I could remember was the one that had arrived before I'd been kidnapped and before the fake policeman had showed up at my apartment. Someone had sent a man to my house, disguised as a policeman, to warn me to be more careful. At the time I thought nothing of it, but I now believed the policeman was connected to Steve and Larry in some way and whoever was controlling them. I scribbled on the notepad before jotting down the message as I remembered it. *Beauty and Charm. One survives. One is destroyed. What are your odds?*

The second note I could remember had been on the beach next to us when we'd awakened, tied together. *Without the truth, there is no answer. In pain, there is darkness. In light, there is nothing. Your bodies are now one, but not as united as they will be by the time I'm done.* I was pretty sure I'd remembered that word for word. The notes were almost etched in my brain—I'd thought of nothing else for so many days.

"How's it going?" Jakob gazed down at me and I just nodded. I was still hurt and didn't want to look at him or say anything right now.

What were the next notes we'd received? It was when we were in the creepy hut. Mine read, *Your life may be saved in death*, and Jakob's note said, *Everyone has a price. Every action has a consequence.* Then Steve had given me a note—at the time I'd thought he'd been trying to warn me away from Jakob, but was he up to something more sinister? That note had read, *Be careful of who you trust and fall in love with. They are deceiving you. You should run away as soon as you can.* I frowned as I scribbled that note down. It didn't seem to fit with the other notes.

Along with the note in the hut I'd found a photo of my

family. Scrawled on the back of the photo was *What do you see when you look at me? A happy family for all to see. A man so consumed with greed and with spite that his children now suffer and live in fright. What do you see when you look at me? An ominous picture of your life to be.* I bit my lower lip as I wrote that down. The words on the back seemed to confirm that my mother was a cheat. Or at least that's the only way I could think to interpret it. Had my mother cheated on my father because he'd been a workaholic? I couldn't remember what my father was like before my mother died. The only other note I had was the letter from my father, and I was scared to reread that and think about what his words might mean now I had more information.

"You okay, Bianca?" Jakob's voice was gentle.

"I was just thinking about my mom and if she cheated on my dad." I gave him a short smile. "I was just wondering what her motivations would have been? Why did she cheat?"

"Sometimes people don't need a motivation."

"There's always a motivation." I shook my head. "If there's one thing I've learned in history, there is always a reason for an action. It might not be a good reason, but one always exists."

"I suppose you're right." He nodded in agreement.

"Here, read this." I handed him the notepad. "These are the clues I can remember. I only have to add my dad's letter to that list." I paused. "And any other notes you have."

"Don't be mad at me, Bianca." He sighed as he held the notepad in his hand. "I didn't know if I could trust you."

"Yet you expected me to trust you from the beginning?" I knew I should just let go of it, but I couldn't stop myself from moaning on.

"I don't know what I expected." He shrugged his shoulders. "Certainly not this, none of this."

"I know." I took a deep breath and squeezed his upper arm. "I'm sorry. I'm going to try and stop bringing up the past as it relates to us."

"Thank you." He leaned over and kissed my forehead.

"So what do you think?" I asked as he read my notes.

"I think you have a good memory." He looked at me with a new light in his eyes. "And not just for obscure movie references."

"Don't hate me because I'm fabulous." I grinned and he laughed.

"The day we met at the coffee shop? That wasn't an accident." He opened his box. "There was a letter sent to me that told me to go to the coffee shop every day until I saw the woman in the photo, and then I was to sit at the table with her."

"And do what?" I frowned.

"It didn't say." He sighed.

"So you just went because a note told you to go?"

"It told me to go if I wanted to find out the truth about my mother's death."

"How did your mother die?"

"She killed herself." His expression changed and I felt my skin grow cold.

"I'm so sorry." I looked away from him. Had my mother driven his mother to her death?

"It's not your fault." He grabbed my hands. "It was my father's fault. I never should have put the blame on anyone else. He was responsible for her death. He's the one that should have paid. Him and him alone."

"I just can't believe my mother would have cheated." My voice cracked in dismay. "It breaks my heart. My dad must have been heartbroken."

"That's why it's best to never let one person mean so much to you that you don't know how to cope if they betray you."

"That's a sad way to live." I gazed at him with sorrowful eyes. How could I have his heart if his heart wasn't there to give?

"It's the best way to live." He shrugged. "You won't ever carry around the burden of a broken heart."

"Your mother was really devastated, wasn't she?" I sighed. "Do you think she had anything to do with my mother's death?"

"Are you asking me if I think our mother's deaths are connected?" he said quietly, his eyes bleak.

"No, I'm sorry. I don't know what I'm asking." I shook my head and looked away in shame. How could I ask him that? And how could he answer?

"It's a fair question." He collapsed onto the couch. "All my life I've wondered—why did my mother let my father affect her for so many years? Yes, he abandoned her. Yes, he cheated on her. But she had me. Wasn't I enough? Was her heartbreak so strong that she couldn't survive for me? I've wanted to know for so many years what drove her to that point. And now here you are and you've got the same questions. 'Why did my mother die?' Maybe their deaths *are* connected." He froze for a moment, his face rigid.

"I guess when you really love someone . . ." I squeezed his hand. "Are you okay, Jakob?"

"The more I think about it, the less sure I am of her heartbreak—or at least the reason for her heartbreak."

"What do you mean?"

"My father was a jerk. My mother knew he was a jerk. She did everything in her power to make it so I wasn't dependent on him or his money. She did everything to make me rise above him and to be successful on my own. She never tried to use me to get closer to him. She never pushed me to make contact with him for her own reasons."

"Hmmm." I leaned back. "Yeah, that doesn't make sense, if she was as obsessed with him as you thought. If she loved him so much, you would think she'd try any excuse to win him back. And a baby is a huge excuse."

"Exactly." Jakob turned toward me and frowned. "Her hatred of my father was real. Her heartbreak was real. The pain she carried around with her was real. I always blamed that heartbreak and pain on the fact that your parents had ruined her relationship with my dad. If only your parents had backed out of their lives. I felt like they ruined everything. First your dad convinced my dad not to marry my mom and then your mom slept with my dad. In a way, I was glad she cheated on your dad because I felt like it was revenge for your dad convincing my dad my mom wasn't good enough. But something has been bothering me. Something doesn't really add up, you know. My mom hated your parents so much, and yet there was always guilt in her eyes when she talked about how she'd been wronged. I never thought about that before. Maybe because I was so focused on my memories of her talking about your mom and your dad ruining her life. And maybe they did have something to do with the pain she carried around. But maybe it was what she did *after* her relationship with my dad that caused her the real heartbreak. Maybe that was the deep shame and sorrow she carried around with her, until she just couldn't anymore. Maybe that was why she sometimes dropped to her knees and sobbed and prayed for forgiveness."

"Are you saying what I think you're saying?" My face turned white as I realized the gravity of the situation we were in.

"I think my mother was responsible for your mother's car crash, Bianca." He nodded. "I think my mother killed your mom."

# twelve

Jakob's words resonated in my brain as I lay in bed the next morning. The smell of coffee woke me from sleep, and I gradually stretched my arms out, tiredness still in my body. I opened my eyes slowly and turned to look at Jakob, but he was no longer in the bed with me.

"He's making coffee, duh," I reprimanded myself as I continued to stretch out in his bed. I stared around his room, taking in his style, and smiled at his taste. The paintings on the walls reminded me of Picasso, and stacks of books were on the dresser and bedside table. I loved that the apartment was lived in and not immaculate. It made Jakob so much more relatable. I jumped out of the bed and walked over to the painting that was hanging to the right of his dresser to study it a bit better.

"It's a Picasso." His deep voice sounded behind me as I studied the vibrant colors of the painting.

"No way." I turned to him with a smile and he handed me a cup of coffee.

"Way." He smiled back at me. My heart melted slightly as his eyes crinkled with emotion as he took in my appearance. "Nice to see you as I remember you, for once."

"What does that mean?" I sipped on the black coffee and made a face.

He burst out laughing and looked at the coffee. "I'm guessing you want milk and sugar?"

"Yes, please." I nodded and followed him out of the bedroom. "What did you mean, by the way? About me looking as you remembered."

"Well, your bedhead and sleepy face with no makeup," he explained sheepishly.

I groaned. "Oh, you mean my scruffy look?"

"I mean your adorable look." He stopped and patted my ass as I walked past him.

"I don't know too many people that think scruffy is adorable." I rolled my eyes, but couldn't stop myself from grinning.

"How did you sleep?" he asked tenderly as he passed me a carton of milk and a bowl filled with sugar cubes.

"Good, thank you." I nodded awkwardly. I had slept soundly, but now I felt uneasy. Not because I was worried about what he might do to me. I was worried about what we might find out and how that would affect us. I felt selfish for thinking it, but a part of me wanted to forget the investigation and just be with Jakob like a normal girlfriend—but we were both in way too deep now.

"I wish I could go back." He sighed and opened the fridge. "Want some toast?"

"Sure." I nodded as he pulled some slices of bread out and put them in a bright red toaster.

"I wish I could meet you under usual circumstances and ignore the notes." He pulled some plates out of a cupboard.

"Why?"

"So everything wouldn't be so complicated. So we could be a regular couple and our only issue would be where we wanted to go to dinner on a Friday night."

"I doubt that would be our only issue." I laughed, then paused as my heart skipped a beat. "And what do you mean 'a regular couple'?"

"I mean normal, no kidnapping issues, no parental murders, no I-kissed-your-brother issues."

"Jakob." I glared at him.

He held his hands up. "Sorry." He made a face. "I know I need to get over that."

"What do you mean by 'normal' couple?"

He took the toast out of the toaster and buttered it. "Like I said, a couple that doesn't—"

"But we're not a couple. We're not together."

"Oh? Since when?" He frowned and handed me a plate.

"What do you mean 'since when'?" I mumbled, confused as hell. Had I been asleep for months or something? Was this some weird *Sleeping Beauty* moment I'd missed or something?

"Since when are we not a couple?" He munched on his toast and stared at me, his eyes sparkling like diamonds.

"Since when are we?" I took a bite of toast and stared back at him.

"Oh." He grinned. "I guess you want this to go the old-fashioned way?"

"What old-fashioned way?"

"Bianca London, will you be my girlfriend?" He leaned forward and licked some crumbs off my lips.

I swallowed hard. "Well, if you're asking . . . ," I mumbled breathlessly.

"I'm asking." He smiled.

"I suppose so," I murmured, excitement coursing through me. Was this real?

"Hmm, no need to sound so excited about it, Bianca." Jakob laughed drily.

"I'd love to be your girlfriend," I said shyly. "I'm just a little taken aback." I grinned at him.

"That's settled, then." He grinned and made a face. "At least one item of ten billion is settled."

"Don't you think it's a bit fast?" I asked softly, wanting more from this moment than a piece of toast and a *that's settled*.

"What's a bit fast?"

"This whole boyfriend-and-girlfriend thing. I mean, you haven't even told me when you started to have feelings for me or what you think of me or where you think this is going or what happens next or anything," I blurted out.

He groaned. "Oh no, you're a typical girl, aren't you?" He grinned at my frown and sat next to me at the kitchen table. "Okay, here goes: I thought you were cute the first time I saw you in the coffee shop, I had inappropriate thoughts of you when we were locked in the back of the car. When I told you about my mother on the island, I knew I wanted to be in a relationship with you. I don't know where this is going. I don't know what's going to happen next. I don't believe in marriage. I'm of two minds about true love and soul mates, and I'm not the sort of guy who's going to want to talk about our relationship every weekend."

"Okay." I looked down, feeling slightly disappointed.

"That *okay* didn't sound too enthusiastic." He grimaced.

"Well, did you expect it to be? No one would exactly call you a romantic." I rolled my eyes and sipped on my coffee.

"Bianca, the first time I saw your face I was taken aback by the feelings that invaded my body. It was the first time I'd ever been drawn to someone just with a glance. When I sat down at the table with you, you made me laugh as you mumbled to yourself, and I knew right away that you were someone different, someone special. As I got to know you on the island, I was attracted to your body and to your brain and I have been captivated by you ever since. There has not been a morning that I've awoken since meeting you that I haven't thought about you. This is a bloody mess of a situation and I'm a bloody mess of a man and I don't know what's going to happen. I wish I could promise you a happily ever after. I wish I could sing sweet nothings into your ear, but I can't. I don't know what's going to happen. Our pasts are so intertwined. Our whole histories are opposed. Even now, we're both seeking the truth and vengeance for our families. How can we live with each other if we're the products of the people who brought each other down?" He stroked the side of my face.

I could feel tears falling from my eyes as I turned to him. "So why even bother asking me to be your girlfriend?"

"Because I wanted you to know for one brief moment, before everything exploded and got bad again, that I really care about you. I want you to know that in a perfect world we'd be together and we'd be happy. That's what I wish we could have. I want it to be as simple as Bianca and Jakob, Jakob and Bianca—but it's never going to be that way for us."

"It could be," I whispered, and grabbed his hand. "We could forget everything. We could just move on and pretend nothing ever happened. We could tell David that—"

"Bianca." Jakob closed his eyes. "We will never be able to forget this and just move on. There are still so many unanswered questions. We owe it to ourselves and each other to figure this all out."

"Even if it ruins us?"

"We didn't have a beautiful beginning." He shrugged. "It seems only natural that we won't have a beautiful ending."

"So we just settle for a beautiful middle?"

"No." He leaned forward and kissed me hard, his eyes burning into mine. "We settle for an explosive middle. We settle for a middle that makes up for the end of the world. We settle for a middle that we can carry to our graves."

"I'm scared, Jakob." I kissed him back. "What are we going to find out?"

"I wish I knew." His eyes darkened and he held my hands. "I just want you to remember that I never intended to hurt you. I never intended for any of this to happen."

"I know." I nodded. And I did. A new honesty was in Jakob's eyes, one I'd never seen there before. True emotion shone through from his soul to mine. Whatever we found out together might break us apart forever, but it wasn't either of our faults. We were innocent parties caught up in the webs our parents had weaved. "I loved my father," I said tenderly. "I loved my father so much, but I wish he'd let this all die with him." I rubbed the tears from my eyes. "I wish he'd just let me be."

~

"Blake's calling me." I grabbed my ringing phone from the coffee table and answered the question in Jakob's eyes as he stared at me.

"Okay." He pursed his lips slightly, and I knew that for all his talk, he still wasn't happy that Blake and I were friends.

"Hey, what's up?"

"You're not going to believe what I found." Blake's voice bounded with excitement through the phone and I smiled.

"Tell me!" I said eagerly, and moved away from Jakob,

whose finger was running down my arm and making its way to my breast. "Stop," I hissed at him as he sat up and leaned forward to kiss me.

"What?" Blake sounded confused, and Jakob grinned at me in response.

"Sorry, not you. What did you find?"

"Seems our good old friend Steve is pretty well connected."

"Connected? With who?"

"So there are photographs of Steve as a boy with many different executives from the Bradley Corporation."

"Yeah, that makes sense." I felt slightly disappointed at his report. That was nothing new. "Hold on, Blake. Hey, Jakob, how did you and your brother know Steve?"

"He was an intern for my dad when he was a teenager." Jakob continued playing with my breasts as he spoke. "He's been with the company for a while. My dad trusted him a lot and he's been on the payroll for many years."

"You're with Jakob, aka Mattias?" Blake's voice was low. "Are you joking?"

"I'm with Jakob, yes, but he's not Mattias, Blake. In fact, there is no Mattias." I sighed, not wanting to have to tell the whole story. "They made Mattias up."

"They made Mattias up?" Blake was in awe. "Like Parcher in *A Beautiful Mind*?"

"Yeah, though they told me Tyler Durden in *Fight Club*."

"Holy shit! Let me get this straight—Mattias Bradley is a figment of the imagination? Was Jeremiah Bradley crazy? Did he have split personality? Manic disorder? Did he suffer from paranoid schizophrenia?"

"Blake, he just made up a fake kid to help protect his real kid from gold diggers," I said, aware that Jakob was listening intently to every word of the conversation.

"Oh, okay, not as exciting then."

"So anything else on Steve, aside from the fact that he was tight with the Bradleys?"

"Bianca, he wasn't just tight with the Bradleys. He was tight with your father as well."

"What?" I fell back against the couch, shaking my head. "That doesn't make sense. How do you know that?"

"How does he know what?" Jakob's eyes searched mine. "What did he say?"

"Blake says that Steve was friends with my father as well."

"Are you sure you want to tell Jakob everything I tell you?" Blake asked warily. "Are you sure we trust this guy?"

"I trust him." I gave Jakob a quick smile.

"If you're sure . . ." Blake sounded uncertain.

"I am. Anything else?"

"Yeah." Blake's voice got excited again. "So Steve lives in a shitty apartment in Washington Heights, right?"

"I guess, if that's what you've found."

"But guess what? About two years ago, he started renting a house in Jersey City. A house that costs way more than his apartment in Washington Heights."

"So?" I took a deep breath. "How is that relevant?"

"At his apartment in Washington Heights, he has full

cable—I'm talking HBO, Showtime, Cinemax, sports channels, everything."

"Okay."

"And at the house in Jersey, he has no cable, not even basic."

"So?"

"So this seems like a guy who likes TV. Why would he have every channel known to man in one place and nothing in the other?"

"Oh yeah, I guess that doesn't make sense."

"It only makes sense if he's not spending much time in the new place—if he's not home to watch TV, why pay for cable, right?"

"Yeah, I guess so."

"Which then makes us ask the question . . ."

"Who *does* live there?" Jakob was frowning at me and I knew he wanted an update. "So Blake found out that Steve is renting two apartments. One in Washington Heights and one in Jersey."

"Jersey?" Jakob frowned. "No, he definitely lives in Washington Heights. I know this because my father kept trying to get him to move downtown, but he always refused. He said Washington Heights is his home and he would never leave."

"Did you hear that, Blake?"

"Not well—why don't you put me on speaker."

"Good idea." I took the phone away from my ear and pressed the speaker button.

"Still here, sweet pea," Blake answered with a laugh. I saw Jakob frowning as he looked at the phone and then at me.

"Blake, be serious."

"I am." His voice changed. "You know I'm here for you and I will do something really bad to anyone that tries to harm you. I'm like a ninja in the night. You won't hear me coming, but I'll be there."

"Is he threatening me?" Jakob looked at me with a raised eyebrow.

"I guess so." I gave him a small smile. "Blake, enough joking around now."

"I mean it."

"Blake, this is Bianca's boyfriend, Jakob. I know you know about our past, but I am committed to Bianca and finding the truth. I have never hurt her and never will. You have my word on that."

"That's good to hear." Blake sounded less sure of himself and I reached over and gave Jakob a kiss on the cheek.

"You're both very sweet guys, but enough." I laughed lightly. "What else did you find out, Blake?"

"Steve has over a million dollars in cash split among three savings accounts. He has no living family that I can see. Can you corroborate that, Jakob?"

"I don't know about the cash." Jakob frowned. "But I can corroborate that he has no family. Both of his parents died when he was a kid. That's kind of why he gravitated to my father so much. My dad trusted him like a son. That's why

David and I trusted him, that's why I had him come to the island. I thought his allegiance was to me and my family."

"Maybe it is," Blake cut in. "But maybe his allegiance is to David and not to you."

"I don't think that's it," I said. "David seemed legitimately perplexed to find out that Steve had gone rogue and disappeared. I don't think he was behind it."

"Neither do I," Jakob added. "At first when we were on the island, I did wonder if it was my brother, but I've thought about it from every angle and it wouldn't make sense. Not at all. There has to be a third party involved."

"So was he close with anyone else besides my dad and the Bradleys?" I asked stiffly. "And do we know why we think he was close with my dad?"

"He worked with your dad in the new product development department. He was almost like an apprentice."

"How do you know this?" I asked softly.

"The less you know about how I got the information the better. Let's just say that there was some conflict at a company picnic one year."

"What?" Jakob spoke up. "When was this? I don't remember any conflict with Steve."

"He trashed a table and threw some punch bowls on the ground after he got into an argument with the company attorney, Larry Renee," Blake said in a rush. "Someone wanted to press charges, but ultimately they were dismissed."

"Who wanted to press charges?" Jakob and I said at the same time.

"I don't know," Blake said, annoyed. "The police report didn't list the name of who wanted to file the charge, it just said 'complainant.' I think the name might have been whitened out and written over. But get this—" He paused for dramatic effect.

"What?" I said hurriedly, my heart racing at this news.

"Steve wanted to file a countercomplaint. But he wanted to file murder charges."

"*Murder* charges?" My jaw dropped as I stared into Jakob's intense blue eyes. "Who did he say was murdered?" I swallowed hard as I waited for the news. Was this my first outside confirmation that my mother had been murdered?

"He stated, and I quote, 'Jeremiah Bradley had my parents killed and I want him to rot behind bars for his sins.' Crazy right?"

"What happened?" My voice was faint with shock. That was not what I'd expected to hear.

"The charges were dropped. I don't see any open investigation into what he said. It was like he never continued with it."

"If he thought Jeremiah killed his parents, why would he work for him? Why would he become like a son to him?" I shook my head and looked at Jakob to see how he was reacting. "It doesn't make sense."

"It does." Jakob nodded slowly, his brain working in overdrive as we sat there. "It makes perfect sense if he wasn't really and legitimately interested in being close to the family."

"What do you mean Jakob?" Blake asked curiously. "From

all accounts, he's been working at the Bradley Corporation for years. Maybe he got drunk one day and made the accusations and then sobered up and recanted."

"Or maybe he realized that the police didn't believe him and the courts weren't the way to get justice." Jakob looked thoughtful. "Maybe he's been playing my family all these years. Maybe he's just been waiting on the perfect time to exact his revenge."

"That would explain the hatred he seemed to have for you on the island," I added. "I think that's why I was so shocked to find out he was working for you. There seemed to be no friendliness from him to you at all."

"We were never the best of friends." Jakob made a face. "But I trusted him. I thought he was loyal."

"So you guys think he's been rogue from the beginning?" Blake sounded excited.

"Yes," Jakob said tightly. "I think he must have been."

"So then we need to get to the bottom of his story," Blake continued. "We need to find out why he thought his parents were murdered by Mr. Bradley, why he turned rogue on the island, what he hoped to accomplish, and we need to know what happened at the picnic."

"The picnic? Do you think that's important?" Jakob sounded annoyed. "Don't we have the information we need from that? We know what's in the police report?"

"We know that he had a complaint at the station. We don't know why he got angry in the first place. And we don't know if his anger is also aimed at Bianca."

"Me? Why would he be angry at me?"

"Well, he was close to your dad. . . ."

"Yeah, so?"

"So, if he was faking it with the Bradleys, he might have been faking it with your dad as well."

"I guess."

"And there's one other thing that struck me. . . ."

"Yeah?"

"Remember how you said the lawyer told you that you had a sibling?"

"Yeah?"

"What if that sibling is Steve?" Blake rushed out. "I know it's a long shot, but with the information we have available, it could be highly possible."

"You think Steve is my brother?" My heart slowed and the blood drained from my face. "No, he can't be."

"And there's one last thing," Blake continued. "I don't know if it's important or not."

"What's that?"

"So that third guy that started the company? Maxwell?"

"Yeah?"

"He just disappeared around the same time that Larry Renee started working as the company attorney. And Larry's the attorney who was responsible for cleaning up the Steve mess."

"So you think there's something between Steve and Larry?"

"It would make sense, right? Maybe Larry is the mastermind

behind all of this," Blake spurted out. "Maybe Larry is the one that set this whole thing up. Maybe he's the mastermind, the Hitler or the Stalin, in the operation."

"But Larry is in hiding." I paused. "Or maybe not. Maybe Larry is pretending he's in hiding."

"So we think Steve and Larry could be hiding out together?" Jakob rubbed his forehead. "And if that's correct, why would Larry care to put this whole thing together?"

"That's what we're going to find out." Blake's voice dropped. "I need you guys to go through all the papers Larry gave you once again. Look for anything that can be helpful, and then we're going to try and find Larry. I think once we find Larry, we find Steve. And when we find both of them, we can figure out what's going on."

"How are we going to figure that out? Do you think they're just going to tell us?" I asked in disbelief.

"Maybe with a little help from my friend." Jakob gave me a tight smile.

"Your friend?"

"My Taurus 709 Slim nine-millimeter." Jakob cocked his head. "I find a gun to the head usually gets people talking fast."

~

"I could lie here with you all day." Jakob nuzzled my neck as we spooned on the couch after getting off the phone. I felt his arms tight around my waist as he cuddled me to him.

"So could I," I said happily, as his fingers brushed across my breasts.

"But we need to concentrate now." He pulled away from me and sat up. "It's time to figure out what's going on. Your friend Blake gave us some great information. We need to look through the papers Larry gave you from your dad."

"You know what I was just thinking?" I reached over and brushed a strand of my hair from his face.

"What's that?" Jakob's eyes searched mine.

"What if the papers weren't from my father?"

"You mean all of them?"

"I don't know. All or some." I shrugged. "Larry could have easily planted information into that box that he wanted me to see."

"You're right." Jakob nodded. "And it was Larry who provided all the information to me and David. He told me your mom slept with my dad. He told David about the box in the first place and that we should be worried you were coming to take down the company."

"He seems to be the common thread in everything that's going on." I nodded. "Which makes me question the paperwork he told me to search through so diligently. What does he want me to find?"

"Let's go through the papers again and notate anything we think could possibly be related and then think about whether it was planted for a reason."

"Yeah, I guess we can do that." I sighed. "Though, I've

been through those papers pretty thoroughly." I held my hands up in despair. "I don't understand why he would plant that. It basically says that my father was one of the founders of the company when it started. It says that he created the products and had the patents. And that he wanted to leave the company and take his patents with him. For some reason he never left, he never got his patents, and we both know he had no power at the company and made very little money. What could Larry possibly want me to take from that, that could benefit him?" I was confused.

"It doesn't add up," Jakob agreed. "If anything, it informs and educates you and puts him and the company in a bad light."

"Yeah, and the letter from my dad, well, that basically informed me that my mom was murdered. Why would he let me have that letter? Why would he want me to know that information?"

"I don't know." Jakob frowned. "But there has to be a reason. And the fact that he told you to look through the paperwork again—he wants to make sure that you understand the importance of all the claims."

"Why would he care?"

"Is there anything else you haven't told me? Any other papers? Any other notes? Any secret files from your father?" Jakob cocked his head and surveyed my face.

"No, not that I know of. Why?"

"We need to speak to Larry. Do you have his number?"

"I don't know where he is—my messages just go to voice

mail now." I sat up as well. "When I spoke to him, his wife called a number from a pay phone. She wouldn't let me have it. He hung up when I was speaking to him, and when we called right back, the line had been disconnected. I don't know what happened, but he sounded really scared. I think he was trying to tell me that there was no Mattias as well." I stared at Jakob, something bothering me. "But if he's the one behind it, why did he sound scared?"

"He might have been on a pay-as-you-go phone." Jakob licked his lips and I was momentarily distracted by the tip of his tongue as it glided back and forth. "If the credit on his phone ran out during the call, it would have disconnected and you wouldn't have been able to get him on the phone again until he added more."

"I never thought about that." My mind was buzzing. "But it makes sense. I was wondering how a phone could just be out of service that quickly." I played with my hair. "So he really was playing me then?"

"He knows all the secrets of the company, Bianca. He knew that there was no Mattias, of course he was playing you," Jakob answered me, his face looking thoughtful. "He was really close to both our dads. I think he was a part of the corporation from the beginning."

"Oh? I didn't know that." I paused. "Didn't Blake say that the paperwork he found said that Larry started after Maxwell left? Oh, how I wish we could find Maxwell."

"Yeah. I don't know his whole story." Jakob frowned. "I just know that my dad trusted Larry more than anyone else."

"I guess that was good for your dad, not so good for anyone else." I made a face. "I know my dad trusted him as well, but look where that got him. A dead wife, no shares in a multibillion-dollar corporation, and a horrible life."

"It doesn't make sense, though." Jakob shook his head as he stared at me. "What did Larry gain?"

"Money, duh." I looked at him for a few seconds, wondering if he was the right person to be investigating this with me. If he couldn't even figure out what Larry was gaining from this, then what sort of smarts did he have?

"Yeah, so that's obvious." Jakob jumped up and ran out of the living room. I stared after him, wondering what was going on. He ran back into the room with the notepad and pen. "Money was his motivator when he was young, but what's his motivation now?"

"He doesn't want to go to jail." I rolled my eyes. "He's trying to scare me off."

"No." Jakob shook his head. "That doesn't make sense. If that were true, he wouldn't have given you the boxes or the information in the first place. He also wouldn't have given you warnings."

"He's the one who told David that I wanted shares in Bradley Inc. He's the one who tipped David off that I was investigating."

Jakob's eyes narrowed. "He was, but why?"

"Like I said, to protect himself."

"Yes, maybe. It doesn't completely add up."

"None of this adds up." I sighed. "The fact is that I only

got into the meeting because I used his proxy shares, so I didn't even have access to be a threat or to seek out your brother until he gave it to me."

"There has to be a reason he gave you your father's paperwork and gave you those shares." Jakob scratched his head. "He could have avoided all of this."

"Yeah, I know what you mean."

"If he hadn't given you the boxes and your dad's letter, you never would have been suspicious of your mother's death. You would have continued on with your life and gone about your business. You never would have wanted to meet Mattias or David Bradley. You never would have wanted to go to the shareholders' meeting. You never would have wanted to investigate your mother's death or your dad's claims."

"Yeah, so what's your point?"

"So there was a reason you were given the boxes. Just like there was a reason I was told to go to the coffee shop." He nodded his head in excitement. "We've all been set up from the beginning to play a part in some grander scheme."

"What grander scheme, though?"

"I don't know." He sighed. "We have to talk to Larry."

"I told you, I don't know how to find him."

"Let's go and see his wife then. Maybe she's heard from him."

"I doubt she's going to want to see me."

"Then I'll talk to her." He jumped off the couch and walked toward his bedroom. I got up and followed him and watched as he walked to his closet, pulling out a shirt and pants. "You need to borrow anything?" He looked back at me.

"No, thanks. I have my own clothes, remember?" I shook my head and opened my bag.

"Oh, darn." He grinned. "It would be nice to see you in one of my shirts again."

"Maybe tonight." I winked at him.

He walked over to me with a devilish look. "Promise?"

"Sure." I giggled, feeling lighthearted as I flirted.

"I can't wait to peel it off of you."

"Pervert." I shook my head at him, my heart racing.

He laughed. "Only for you, Bianca. Only for you."

"I'm sure you say that to all the girls," I teased as he kissed me lightly on the nose. My stomach flipped as he held me close to him. His body pressed into mine, and if I closed my eyes, I could pretend we were back on the island. Just the two of us.

"All the girls don't matter." He stroked my hair and I could feel his heart beating in his chest. We stood there for a few minutes, both of us knowing that this was our safe haven.

"Why did you let me just leave the island?" I looked up at him curiously. "I haven't been able to figure it out."

His eyes were dark. "I knew there was no point trying to keep you there against your will if you didn't trust me. So I let you go."

"Why did you let me go before the merger went through?" I asked him softly. "How did you know I wouldn't try to stop it?"

"I didn't know it hadn't gone through as yet." He looked away from me. "I was taken aback when I found that out." He turned back to me and grabbed my hands. "Bianca, I want you to know that I don't care what you do about the merger. This was never about money for me." He stepped back and gazed into my eyes.

"But it was for David, wasn't it? That's what was in the kidnapping for him? Me being gone for the merger to go through?" I stared at Jakob, just thinking. The whole dynamic between David and Jakob still didn't add up, not completely. They distrusted each other so much. And David had kept asking me about Jakob as if he wasn't sure of Jakob's moves. How could they have planned this together if they couldn't stand each other?

"David is greedy, he always has been," Jakob said. "Ever since he was a little boy, all he thinks about is money and the company. That's what Jeremiah Bradley stood for at the end of the day, money and power—and it's what David inherited."

"I still can't believe he made up another person to pretend that he had nothing to do with the company." I shook my head. "I can't believe he fooled me so well. I had no idea that he had any business acumen."

"You had no idea at all?"

"No." I bit my lower lip. "But only because that's what he kept telling me. I should have realized he was trying to throw me off the scent." I sighed. "I should have realized that there was no Mattias Bradley." I looked at Jakob keenly to see how he reacted to my statement. I wanted to be 100 percent positive that there was no Mattias Bradley.

"He was nothing but a figment of the imagination." Jakob looked into my eyes. "A name made up by my father to protect my brother and his interests."

"Why the name Mattias?"

"Have you ever heard of Saint Matthias?"

"No." I shook my head.

"He was the apostle chosen after Judas betrayed Jesus and he was crucified."

"Okay." I looked at Jakob blankly. "What does that mean?"

"He became the twelfth apostle, chosen by God after the apostles prayed to him for guidance. There were two men for them to choose from. It was between Matthias and a guy called Joseph, also know as Barsabbas. Both men had been with Jesus through his whole ministry, and ultimately Matthias was chosen. Such an important role he played, but he was only mentioned in the Bible once. But the most important part of the story is that Matthias was with them every step of the way, even before he was chosen. He witnessed the ministry of John the Baptist and he witnessed Christ's ascension."

"So?"

"So my dad liked his story. And he wanted to choose a name that represented something powerful. Mattias was created to protect my brother and his assets. Mattias was created and entrusted by God, that's what my father liked to think."

Jakob shrugged and gave me a smile. "I take it you're not a religious person?"

"I never went to church growing up and I've never read the Bible." I made a face. "Are you religious?"

"I never talk religion or politics with friends." He winked at me. "I don't like to lose them."

"I didn't ask you to talk religion or politics. I asked you if you were religious."

"I believe in God, let's leave it at that." He took a step back. "And with that we should get going. Hopefully, Larry's wife can help us."

"Yeah." I frowned. Why was Jakob being so evasive? I thought we were finally past that. I was about to ask him more about the creation of Mattias when his phone rang.

"Jakob Bradley," he barked. "What?" His voice was cold and his eyes narrowed as he gazed at me. "Are you sure?"

"What's going on?"

He held a finger up to me. "Shit!" he exclaimed angrily, and hung up.

"What's going on, Jakob?" I frowned

He grabbed my hand and pulled me into the living room. He grabbed his remote control and turned the TV to CNN. My jaw dropped as I gazed at the breaking news headline on the screen: *Top New York Lawyer Busted for Tax Fraud and Evasion Expected to Blow the Whistle on Several Billionaires.*

"Oh my God," I whispered as I stared at the screen. Larry Renee was in handcuffs, being walked to some cars surrounded by police. "What's going on?" I looked at Jakob, who was standing there with his fists clenched and his jaw tight.

"What's going on here?" He turned to me with a frown. "We just lost access to the man who could put all the pieces of the puzzle together." He stared at me for a few seconds. "This puts all of our theories into jeopardy. Larry Renee is looking less and less like the kingpin here. And that also means he's not likely to lead us to Steve."

"Can't we go and visit him in jail?"

"He's not going to county jail, Bianca." Jakob pulled his phone out again. "He's been taken in by the Feds. He has big-name clients. They're going to want him to spill. They're not going to give him access to anyone but an attorney." Jakob banged his fist against his thigh. "Shit."

"What are we going to do?" I could feel that my whole body had gone cold. "How did they even find him?"

"That's what I want to know." Jakob glanced at me. "I think we need to go see David."

"Are you going to call him?" I looked at the phone in his hands.

"No." He shook his head. "This visit needs to be a surprise."

~

We drove in silence to David's apartment, both of our heads spinning. I held the notepad in my hand and reread the clues over and over as we drove. Then I pulled my father's letter out of my bag and reread it. I stared at the lines in my father's letter that had affected me the most: *I don't think your mother's car crash was an accident . . . there may have been people who wanted to see me incapacitated. People who knew that your mother's death would change everything.*

He had said *people*, so that meant that more than one person was involved in my mother's death. I sighed—that obviously meant that it was more than just Jeremiah Bradley, something that hadn't occurred to me before. Then I thought of the last line: *People who knew that your mother's death would change everything.* What people and what did it change? What did my mother's death change? I'd assumed that he'd been talking about himself stepping away from the company due to grief, but that seemed too simple now. Yes, everyone mourns in his or her own way, but most people wouldn't withdraw from society and their stake in a major corporation. How was someone to know that my father would do that?

"Do you think my father knew my mother cheated on him?" I spoke out loud as I thought. "And why would my mother cheat? Didn't she know about the other women as well? She couldn't possibly have thought Jeremiah was going to stay with her. We already know he was hooking up with your mom, and then the lady in the photograph, and then David's mom. That's three other women, and those are just the ones we know about. Why would my mom add herself to the mix?"

"Why do women do what they do?" Jakob shrugged as he pulled up outside David's building.

"I'm going to ignore that comment for now." I shook my head as I got out of the car. "Your dad was the man-whore."

"Is this our first argument, Bianca?" Jakob grinned as he walked up next to me on the pavement.

"I think this is our fiftieth." I laughed.

"But first official one as a couple."

"There will be a second official one in a minute if you don't shut up." I glanced at his laughing eyes and leaned over and kissed him on the cheek. "I must be crazy," I whispered as I reached out and grabbed his hand.

"Let's go inside and see David." Jakob walked me into the building and the doorman nodded at him.

"Good morning, Mr. Bradley."

"Good morning, Joseph. We're just going up to see my brother."

"Certainly, Mr. Bradley." Joseph paused. "He has a guest right now."

"A guest?"

"His girlfriend, Roma." Joseph gave me a look. "I only tell you, sir, because Mr. Bradley had me make a trip to CVS."

"Oh." Jakob paused and then grinned. "I see."

"I just got back ten minutes ago," Joseph continued. "So maybe come back in fifteen minutes?"

"I'll come back in thirty." Jakob laughed and grabbed my hand. "That should be enough time. Come on, Bianca. Let's go get a doughnut."

~

"Speaking of condoms . . . ," Jakob said once we were walking down the street to the doughnut shop.

"Yes?" I could feel my face growing red as he stared at me.

"You and me." He nodded. "You might need to get tested."

"Tested?" I said stupidly, knowing exactly what he was talking about. It had been weighing in the back of my mind as well, but I hadn't wanted to think about it.

"You might be pregnant, Bianca."

"I'm sure I'm not."

"We need to check though, just in case." He squeezed my hand.

"I'll get a pregnancy test, but I'm sure I'm not."

"I don't think this is something you can be sure of." He looked at me as we entered the shop. "We've had sex without protection more than once, Bianca. It's a possibility."

"Shhh." I glared at him as I saw two men staring at us with interest. "Keep your voice down."

"I'm just saying."

"Well, don't just say." I turned away and stared at the doughnuts. "Who is Roma, by the way?"

"I've only met her once." Jakob shrugged. "But she's some girl he's been seeing on and off for a few years."

"You know her name, and you know they've been seeing each other for a few years, but you've only met her once?"

"We're not exactly close." Jakob shrugged. "He never offered for us to hang out more than that and I never cared. She's a pretty girl, but there's something a bit off about her."

"So he was dating her when he was seeing me?" I asked quietly.

"I guess so. Like I said, I don't put my nose in his business."

"So how did you guys work out the kidnapping, then?" I looked at Jakob with intense eyes. "Who figured all of that stuff out? You must have talked."

"At the time we had a mutually beneficial reason to want you gone."

"There's something that doesn't make sense to me." I gazed at him for a few seconds. "I get the box from Larry. Larry warns David that I'm investigating. David knows what I'm doing as soon as we meet at the shareholders' meeting. He knows my dad created several of the inventions. He believes I'm trying find a way to bring down his family company or take my share or whatever."

"Uh-huh."

"So that adds up fine. Even the fact that he contacts you and says he wants you to take care of this problem, to protect your money." I stopped and looked at Jakob carefully. "What I don't get is, who told you to go to the coffee shop? And why? You weren't enticed with money. You were enticed with information. Information about your mother. You were enticed with the truth."

"Yes, so what?"

"So isn't that a huge coincidence? Larry warning David, David warning you, and another party also warning you about the same person, but for totally different reasons?"

"Unless Larry was the one sending the notes." Jakob shook his head. "Though I doubt it. Whoever was sending the notes also had access to Steve. And at this point, I'm not so sure that Larry and Steve are working together."

"Couldn't Larry have had access to Steve? Didn't they both work for Bradley? Maybe Larry and Steve came up with this plan together because . . ." My voice trailed off, as I had nothing to add. What could they possibly hope to gain?

"Yes, but I don't think they ever had much contact." Jakob sighed. "And now that Larry's in jail, it indicates that someone bigger is involved in all of this."

"He was scared of someone, at least he and his wife acted like they were scared of someone." I paused and thought. "Though after we spoke with Blake, I started to think that maybe that was an act and maybe he was the mastermind."

"If Larry was the mastermind, he wouldn't be on his way to jail now, would he?"

"No, I guess not."

"So that means there's someone else pulling the strings."

"Someone like who?" I frowned. "The lady in the photo?"

"I don't think so." Jakob paid for two doughnuts and coffees and we took a seat. "Not if she was begging in the street outside your apartment for so many months."

"Yeah." I sighed. "Then who?"

"It has to be someone important. Someone who has a lot to lose. Someone who enjoys playing games . . . someone like my dad." Jakob watched me over the rim of his coffee cup. "It can't be my dad because he's dead, so it has to be—"

"Maxwell!" I rushed out. "It has to be the third partner, Maxwell."

"Yes." Jakob nodded slowly. "I'm starting to think you're right. He's the only one left."

"What do we know about him?"

"Well, we know that he left right before Larry started working there." Jakob frowned. "Though I could have sworn Larry was with them all from the beginning." He sighed.

"Maybe Maxwell is mad that he had to leave and blames Larry and me?" I sipped on my coffee and nearly choked as I remembered something else. "Larry's wife told me that Maxwell's wife had contacted them." My eyes widened as I remembered. "She said that Maxwell's wife threatened them!"

"How?" Jakob leaned forward. "What did she do?"

"I don't know." I shook my head. "I was more concerned with getting to talk to Larry, so I didn't really follow up with that. Man, I suck."

"It's fine, Bianca. We're new to this. We can't expect to be CIA operatives in ten minutes."

"Yeah, I guess. I wish I knew more." I closed my eyes for a few seconds and tried to take deep breaths.

"I don't know anything either, but I know a man who does." I heard Jakob's chair scrape along the floor as he jumped up. "Come on, we're going back to David's."

"But I thought he was having sex with Roma." I opened my eyes and made a face, not wanting to walk in on David fornicating again.

"I don't give a shit." Jakob hurried me out of the restaurant. "I think my dear brother has more information than he let on before. I think this is about more than money to him. I think this is a game as well."

"Why do you say that?"

"What he tried to do to you earlier." Jakob's voice was angry. "He was trying to rile me up."

"What do you mean?"

"He chose George to pick you up that night. George was my driver for many years. He's loyal to me. David knows that. He *wanted* George to call me and tell me what was going on that night. He wanted me to drive over to his house that night. He wanted me to see the two of you together." Jakob started walking faster. "I think we've both been played, Bianca."

"But why?"

"That's what we're going to find out."

# thirteen

"How did he leave so fast?" I frowned as Jakob and I left the building and headed for his car.

"Almost as if he were tipped off." Jakob drove off.

"You think Joseph told him?"

"I think there was no CVS trip." Jakob nodded.

"Why didn't we ask Joseph?"

"He'd deny it." Jakob slammed his hand against the steering wheel. "Fuck!"

"What are we going to do now? We don't have access to Larry. We don't know who Maxwell is. David's gone into hiding. We don't know who the lady in the photograph is. What do we have?"

"We have Steve." Jakob sounded thoughtful. "We know he was working for someone who wanted to intimidate both of us. And at this point, I don't think it was Larry."

"You don't think he was working for David?"

"No." Jakob shook his head. "His loyalties were stronger to me than to David."

"But he turned on you."

"Yes, he did. But I refuse to believe it would be for someone like David. He couldn't stand rich kids who've been handed everything on a silver platter. He wouldn't have done this for David, and I don't think that David would have hired him anyway. What would David care if we got close? Why would he want us both intimidated?" Jakob shook his head. "It doesn't make sense. At first, I thought it had to be David. That's why I pretended to be Mattias when you accused me. I wanted you to think you'd caught me out. I wanted you to think you knew everything."

"Why?"

"Because I knew that if you knew that there was no Mattias, you'd keep digging. And I didn't want you in any more danger. Not when I knew someone was out there trying to scare us both."

"You were worried about me?"

"I didn't even want to let you go, but I knew you wouldn't trust me. My best bet was to let you think I was Mattias and let you go home."

"But you couldn't stay away. You still texted and called me and left that weird note."

"I texted and called you because I had to be in contact with you. I didn't leave you any note."

"Yes, you did, the night you snuck into my apartment."

"I only snuck into your apartment the night we had sex." He looked at me with a worried frown.

"You didn't cross out *Jakob* and write *Mattias* on a letter?" I asked, perplexed, my brain working fast. "The person hadn't broken in. They had to have had a key."

"Who has a key?"

"Well, you do. How else did you get in?"

"I was given a copy of your keys . . . by David."

"What? Why would he do that? And how did he have them?"

"I assumed you'd given him a copy?"

"No. He never even came to my place." I shook my head and then gasped. "Do you think he snuck into my apartment that night?"

"Possibly." Jakob nodded. "But not because of you, because of me."

"Because of you?"

"He wanted to bring me out into the open. He knew I'd find out and he knew that I'd have to get involved again."

"What do you mean?"

"When I let you return, I came back as well, but I didn't tell him. I knew he'd want to know what had happened, but I no longer trusted him. He must have realized that something had gone wrong when you called him from the hotel. We were meant to be on that island for two to three weeks. That was the original plan. He obviously knew you'd arrived back, and he was calling me, demanding to know what was going on. I didn't answer him. I needed time to think. I think

David realized that and he was trying to get to you. I think that's why he was trying so hard to turn you against me and convince you I was Mattias and couldn't be trusted. He knew when I didn't contact him when I got back that I was onto him. After Steve went rogue, I knew that there was a lot more going on than I'd thought."

"You keep saying that! Why didn't you tell me that when we were on the island?"

"Would you have wanted to listen to me then? You didn't trust me. And obviously it was for a good reason. I needed to regain your trust by letting you go. I needed you to know that I never had any intention of harming you in any way."

"I wish you'd at least tried to tell me."

"I'm sorry." He reached over and squeezed my hand.

"I have a question for you about the company."

"Sure."

"So this merger that's about to go through, do you think that's the only reason David wanted me gone?" I sighed. "I don't understand why he didn't try and kidnap me again when I returned, if he'd wanted me out of the way so badly. The merger hasn't gone through yet, has it?"

"The merger goes through tomorrow," Jakob muttered.

"Where do you think David went?"

"No idea." Jakob sighed. "I think our best right now is to go back to my place and look at the clues again."

"Why does it feel like we keep going around in circles? Every time we want to talk to someone they disappear."

"That's why I'm not letting you out of my sight. I don't want you to disappear again."

"Well, you were the one that kidnapped me last time. Maybe it's you I should be worried about."

Jakob shot me a look, but he didn't answer. Instead he turned on the radio. Lady Gaga's "Bad Romance" blasted out of the speakers. Was the universe having a laugh at my expense? Or just sending me a message?

I answered the phone on the first ring, wondering who was calling me from a blocked number. I looked at the bathroom door and wondered if I should call Jakob out of the shower so he could hear the call as well, but decided against it.

"Hello?"

"Bianca, I need to talk to you."

"Larry?" I could hear the shock in my voice.

"Are you alone?" he whispered hurriedly.

"Yes, why?"

"You cannot repeat this to anyone. You're the only one I trust."

"What's going on, Uncle Larry?" I'd slipped into calling him uncle again, even though I no longer considered him family.

"Bianca, I've been set up."

"Sure." I sighed. "Larry, your lies aren't going to work now. I know you told David about me wanting the shares."

"Listen to me, Bianca. I admit I've made mistakes." He

paused. "Please, Officer, may I have a few more minutes?" He sounded worried. "Listen to me carefully, Bianca. I can't talk long. I'm in jail. I've been set up for tax evasion, fraud, and insider information."

"Insider information?" I asked, surprised. "What insider information?"

"You cannot let the merger go through," he said quickly. "You have to stop the merger."

"What are you talking about? Why?"

"The Bradley Inc. merger," he shouted. "He fooled us. I don't know how I missed it, but you have to ensure it's stopped. You have the shares. I took care of it. They're in your name. Go to my house. Go and see my wife. She'll give you the papers. You need to stop it before it's too late."

"What's going on? Who fooled you? Was it Maxwell? Who is Maxwell, Larry? Tell me, who is Maxwell?"

"That's it, Mr. Renee," a voice said in the background. "The call is done."

"Bianca, listen to me! Do not trust Jakob Bradley—and you need to stop that merger. If it goes through, it's all over. It will all be for nothing."

"What will have been for nothing?"

The phone went dead. I looked at the phone in my hands and glanced up guiltily as Jakob came out of his bathroom, hair wet and slick.

"You okay?" He looked at the phone in my hand. "Phone call?"

"Larry called me," I said slowly, staring at Jakob's perfectly chiseled body.

"What did he say?" Jakob rushed over to me, his eyes wide. I stared at the towel around his waist, distracted by the image he made, half-naked and wet as he sat next to me on the bed. "What did he say, Bianca?" His dark eyelashes were moist and his blue eyes were vivid and alert. "Are you okay?" He massaged my shoulders and moved closer to me. I could feel the heat radiating off him.

"He said he was set up," I said finally, not wanting to say anything else. Why had Larry told me I couldn't trust Jakob? Was Jakob looking out for me now or was he trying to set me up?

"Did he ask for your help?"

"He asked me to try and find out what's going on." I nodded. I wasn't going to tell Jakob everything, just in case. Immediately, I felt remorse and guilt. Was I really going to take Larry's word and stop trusting Jakob?

"Is he joking?" Jakob snarled. "Why would you help him after what he's done?"

"I guess he had no one else to call."

"He should call his wife or David."

"Yeah." I nodded, then sat back casually, letting my body fall back into Jakob's. "Do you think I should try and stop the merger now? Do you think I should show my paperwork and see if I can get my rightful shares of the company?"

"No." He shook his head. "I don't."

“Jakob”—I stared at him intently—“Larry told me not to trust you.”

“I see.” He studied my face. “And you believed him?”

“No.” I paused. “For a split second, yes.” I sighed. “For a split second I was confused, but I trust you, Jakob. I would never take Larry’s word over yours. I trust you.”

“I’m glad.” His hands caressed my face as he gazed into my eyes. “Larry’s still playing his games, isn’t he?”

“He wants me to go see his wife. She might have more information for us.”

“Then we shall go and see his wife.” He pulled me toward him hard. “But not until we take care of some unfinished business.”

“Oh?” I gasped as I felt his hardness against my stomach.

His hands cupped my breasts and he squeezed them together. His lips fell to the side of my neck and he kissed me softly. “I love your smell.” He breathed me in, his fingers squeezing my breasts.

“Jakob?” I moaned as his right hand slipped down and made its way into my panties.

“Yes?” His fingers rubbed me gently and I moaned again, slightly louder this time.

“Why do you think Larry asked me to help him?”

“He’s trying to play you again.” Jakob bit my earlobe. “But we’re not dumb, we already know his game.” His left hand pulled my top up and he pushed me down on the bed. “He can rot in hell for all I care.” He kissed me on the forehead, then the nose, then the lips, and made his way down the valley between my breasts before sucking on my right nipple.

"You just showered." I groaned as my back arched involuntarily.

"So?" He moved his hips slightly to pull his towel off, throwing it onto the floor before lowering himself back on top of me. His cock was already hard and erect against me. Streaming kisses down my stomach, he grabbed my panties with his teeth and pulled them down my legs before tossing them to join his towel.

"Jakob," I whimpered as his right hand played in my wetness. "We should be thinking about what to do next. We should be on our way to see Mrs. Renee."

"I know what I want to do next." He grinned before spreading my legs open and lowering his face to my private spot. "I want to do you with my tongue and then my cock. Then we can talk."

"Jakob," I groaned, but his answer was to put his tongue between my legs and to start sucking. "Oh!" I cried out as his tongue slid inside me and he grabbed my hips and pulled me down onto his face harder. "Oooh . . . ," I screamed as his tongue moved back and forth in abandon and licked me up. I could feel my orgasm building up quickly, my mind losing focus on everything else. When he pulled his tongue out of me, I cried out at the loss of him inside me, but he soon rectified that by sliding his hard cock inside me.

"Open your eyes, Bianca," he growled. "I want to see

your expression when I make you come." He thrust into me and groaned. "Shit, you're so wet." He moved his hips faster as he slammed into me. "I can't have enough of you, you know that, right?"

"Shut up and fuck me," I cried out.

He chuckled. "Yes, ma'am." He pulled out of me, pulled me up, and pushed me forward. "Ass back."

"What?" I moaned as he slid into me from behind. "I thought you wanted to see my eyes when I came?"

"I'll watch your face again in a moment. For now, I want you to feel every inch of me inside of you. I want to fuck you so hard and deep that you won't ever forget me."

"Faster!" I screamed as he made his pace more deliberate.

"Nope." He moved even slower, sliding his cock in and out at the pace of a snail before pushing himself in hard right at the end.

"Jakob," I whimpered as my body tingled all over. "Please."

"Please?" He laughed and pulled my hair back. "Kiss me," he commanded, and I turned my face so that he could claim my mouth. Then he pulled all the way out of me and licked his lips before entering me again slowly. "Hold on to the sheets." He chuckled and then increased his pace, so that his cock was flying in and out of me.

"Ooh!" I screamed as I felt myself taken to the top of the cliff. "I'm coming!" I screamed again as I gripped the sheets tightly, cascades of pleasure rippling through my body. "Oh, Jakob."

"Bianca." He grunted as he continued slamming into me,

then I felt his body shuddering as he exploded inside me. He pulled out and fell onto the bed next to me and pulled me into his arms. I stared into his face and closed my eyes, my body feeling exhausted as I cuddled up next to him.

"End act one, scene one." He groaned as he kissed me hard.

"What do you mean?"

"This is where I'd end the scene." He groaned. "This is where I'd end the entire play."

"What play?"

"Nothing." He shook his head and chuckled.

"Who are you, Jakob Bradley?" I asked him quietly. "What's your story?"

"What do you mean?"

"I've been thinking about something and it's been bothering me for a while."

"What's that?" He leaned on his elbow and stared at me.

"You said your mom was a maid for the Bradleys."

"Yes." He nodded.

"You said your mom refused to take money from your dad."

"Yes." He nodded.

"George the doorman knew your mom, and he recognized me because of my mom."

"Yes." Jacob's eyes narrowed.

"Which means that you grew up here. My mom died when I was young, so your mom lived here for a long time. How did she afford it? Where did she get the money?" I looked at his face carefully, but his expression never changed.

"I guess Bradley must have given her money after all?" He shrugged.

"So he wasn't that bad to her then, was he?"

"Well, they were in love for a while." He shrugged. "Maybe he gave it to her as a parting gift, before he married someone else."

"Yes, maybe." I nodded, thinking back to Larry's comment. *You can't trust Jakob Bradley.* I hated to doubt him again after everything and especially because of what Larry had said, but things still weren't adding up.

"Why did you even think of that?" he asked me softly, his fingers running up and down my arm.

"Not sure." I jumped up, suddenly uncomfortable with my own thoughts and doubts. "I should shower."

"I'll join you."

"You don't have to."

"I want to." He smiled sweetly. "Isn't that what couples do? Shower together?"

"Yeah. I guess so."

"We're in this together, Bianca." He came up behind me and his arms encircled my waist. "It's you and me, kid."

"Yeah." I nodded. Oh, how I wanted to believe that.

~

"Let's go see Larry's wife now." I rubbed my body dry and stared at Jakob's reflection in the mirror. "I want to see if there's anything else she didn't tell me before."

"Sure, I think that's a good idea." He nodded and licked

a drop of water off the back of my neck. "But we have to be smart about it. This could be a setup. There has to be a reason Larry wants us to go see her. We need to remember that whatever she says might be for show—but she could know more than she's been letting on. Maybe she knows the real truth behind everything. If she does, then we're going to try our damnedest to figure it out."

"I hope so." I walked into the bedroom. "And I need to call Rosie—she must be worried about me."

"When do I get to meet her?"

"Soon." I thought about Rosie meeting Jakob. She was going to think I was crazy to be dating the man that had kidnapped me, and I couldn't blame her.

"You don't want her to meet me, do you?"

"Well, not right away." I made a face as I pulled my clothes on. "Maybe when all this is sorted out."

"She's your best friend."

"Yes." I nodded.

"Yet she never called the police when you were gone for a week and she's been flaking on you since you've been back, even though she knows you were kidnapped."

"Yes." I sighed. "She thought I left the bar with a guy I'd met and she's dating this guy and, well, I haven't been available. . . ." My voice trailed off as I realized how weak my explanation sounded.

"She doesn't sound like a great friend." He pulled on a shirt. "You ready to go?"

"Yeah." I nodded. "Let's go."

"You know where Larry's wife lives?"

"She lives out on Long Island. I have the address in my bag."

"Okay, then. Bring your notes and we'll go over the clues again and see what we missed."

I grabbed my handbag and we exited his apartment. As we took the elevator down, all I could think about was my own place. I wanted to go back and check up on it. It felt strange to miss it, but in a way I felt that I had betrayed it by staying with Jakob. I missed my space and my bed. I missed just being there.

"You okay?" Jakob squeezed my hand.

"Yeah, I was just thinking about my apartment." I gave him a half smile. "Just hoping no one's gone back there."

"Yeah." He nodded. "We'll have to get your stuff and move it into my apartment."

"What?" My jaw dropped. "What are you talking about?"

"You're moving in with me. I can't let you go back to that place."

"I'm not moving in with you, Jakob, that's way too fast." I shook my head. What was going on here?

"Just for now, until we figure out everything."

"I can't stay with you forever."

"We'll talk about it later. We have bigger concerns to deal with now."

"You're not the boss of me, Jakob. You can't tell me how to live my life."

"Like I said, we'll talk about it later."

"You shouldn't be here." Larry's wife came outside as we were walking up the driveway. "You both need to leave."

"Larry sent me." I walked up to her. "He said you'd have some papers for me." I could feel Jakob's eyes on me. I'd omitted that part, and he wasn't happy about it.

"I don't want to get involved." She looked at Jakob and then back at me.

"Mrs. Renee, please. This is important."

"I told Larry I'm done. I don't want any part of this anymore."

"Any part of what?" Jakob stepped closer to her.

"I never signed up for this life, you know." She looked angry. "When I met Larry, I thought he was a good guy. I didn't know he was married."

"Married?" I looked at Jakob and we exchanged a glance.

"I didn't know." She looked guilty. "I didn't know he was a father, either."

"Father? He has kids?" My eyes widened. "What?"

"He has a daughter." She nodded. "She hates him."

"He has a daughter?" I repeated, my heart beating fast.

"Yes, he didn't have much of a relationship with her until a few years ago." She looked at me. "That's when everything changed. I knew something bad was coming. I just knew it." Her face looked bleak. "I thought it was my payback for ruining a marriage. I thought I deserved the hostility and tension for being a home wrecker, but this is all too much now. His daughter coming back into his life ruined everything."

"Why?" I breathed out.

"Roma was bad news. I could see it in her eyes, the very first time I met her."

"Roma?" Jakob's voice rose and I froze. "Her name is Roma?"

"Yes." Mrs. Renee nodded. "Evil girl she was."

"Where is she now, Mrs. Renee? How do we get in contact with her?"

"I don't know." She shook her head. "She and I are not close. I don't even know where she lives and I don't want to know. I want a divorce from Larry. I'm not letting Larry take me down with him." She took a deep breath. "I suppose it's my penance for splitting up his first marriage. This is the price I had to pay. That's how karma goes. You can't ruin a marriage and expect your marriage to go perfectly."

"I'm sorry. I didn't know."

"It's not something I publicized." She laughed bitterly. "Though in that group of friends it didn't mean much. All of those men were cheats and liars."

"I'm sorry." I could see she was near the breaking point. "Do you have anything for me? Larry said that you might have something to give to me."

She stared at me for a few seconds, her pupils dilating as

she turned around. "Come with me quickly." She walked toward the house, and Jakob and I followed her inside. She walked into the kitchen, grabbed an envelope off the counter, and handed it to me. "Larry said to give this to you. He said you'd know what to do." I took hold of the envelope, but she held on to it tightly without letting it go. "Think carefully before you make your next step, Bianca. There are people watching everything."

"I'll be careful, Mrs. Renee." I nodded. "I promise."

"Don't come back here." She shook her head. "I don't want anything to do with any of this anymore."

"I have one last question for you, please," I begged as she took a step back.

"What is it?" She looked around suspiciously again.

"Do you know anything about Maxwell, the third partner in Bradley, London, and Maxwell?"

She stared at me for a second, her face twisting as she laughed, an odd, loud sound from her petite body.

I recoiled in shock. "Mrs. Renee?"

"They were all thick as thieves, you know. Thick as thieves and too smart for their own good. Not a one of them was good." She glanced at me and then at Jakob. "Not a one of them."

"Not a one of who?" I asked quietly.

"Not Bradley, not London, and not Maxwell." She shook her head. "What a twisted, twisted web they wove."

"But what about Maxwell?" I ignored her comments about my father. I didn't even want to know what she was talking about. She didn't know my father. My father was a good man. My father had been cheated on. He'd been devastated. He had tried the best that he could.

"Maxwell got the last laugh, didn't he?" She chuckled. "He screwed us all."

"What are you talking about?" I could feel my heart racing. "How did he screw us all?"

"What *are* you talking about, Mrs. Renee?" Jakob took a step forward and grabbed her wrist. "Tell us what you mean."

"You're Jakob Bradley." She batted her eyelashes at him. "How ironic that you're here with her." She laughed.

"Mrs. Renee." Jakob's voice grated like a knife in the air and his expression was hostile, even arrogant, as he stared at her.

"Mrs. Renee, why did Maxwell's wife contact you both and threaten you?" My voice cut through the tension in the room. She looked at me blankly. "When I was here last time, you said that Maxwell's wife had threatened you." She glanced at me again for a second without speaking, then turned to face Jakob again.

"My husband was the one who decided on the name Mattias," she said softly. "It wasn't your father. My husband had a thing about names. He liked to be clever."

"Mrs. Renee—" Jakob started again.

She squared her shoulders and looked at both of us with sad eyes. "That's my name." She nodded her head. "You both need to leave now. Good-bye." She turned around and walked back to the front of the house.

"Should we—" I started.

Jakob cut me off as we walked down the corridor and through the front door. Mrs. Renee slammed it behind us without another word.

"What's in the envelope?" He pulled the envelope out of my hands.

"What are you doing?" I frowned and tried to grab it back.

"What's in the envelope?" He glared at me and ripped it open. "Why didn't you tell me we were coming here for a purpose?"

"I didn't know if you would think it was a good idea, what with not trusting Larry at all."

"I don't trust Larry, and I don't think that whatever is in the envelope is there for good intentions."

"Who knows what to think now? Why did you just let us leave without interrogating Mrs. Renee a bit more?" I put my hand out. "Give me back my papers. What do they say?"

"First, Mrs. Renee was close to a breakdown. I don't even think she knows what side she's on right now. Trust me, I'm not done with her, but we need to give her some time. And we need to find something on her to make sure she gives us the information we need. Secondly, these are papers saying you own a thirty-five percent share in Bradley Inc." He looked at the papers and handed them back. "Why do you have papers giving you a thirty-five percent share in my family's company?"

"So I can stop the merger." I repeated what Larry had

asked me to do. "Larry told me to use these papers so that I can stop the merger from going through."

"You can't stop the merger, Bianca." Jakob shook his head. "Don't you find it suspicious that out of the blue Larry has now provided you with papers giving you a major stake in the company?"

"I don't know. Maybe he's realized the error of his ways. Maybe he's trying to make amends? Why shouldn't I use the shares and stop the merger?"

"What if these shares are a setup?"

"What if they aren't? If the merger goes through, I might not get anything." I thought back to what I'd read in the newspaper.

"You have a claim to Bradley Inc. in your hand now, Bianca." Jakob's voice was intense. "You can share in any profits that the company receives from the merger."

"I didn't think of that." I gasped.

"And I think that Larry was hoping that wouldn't cross your mind as well. He made a mistake giving you the shares. For some reason he wants you to stop the merger because it's in his best interests, not yours."

"I don't know what to do."

"What is it that you want?"

"I want what my father worked hard for."

"Do you think Larry would just hand you your shares out of the kindness of his heart?" Jakob asked me grimly. "Do you think that after all this it would be this simple?"

"I don't know." I sighed deeply. Why did Larry care about

me getting the shares? How would this help him? "I don't think he would hand me the shares after all these years out of the kindness of his heart, not really."

"Think, Bianca. Please. This could be a setup."

"How? What sort of setup is giving me my rightful shares? Maybe he knew that he was about to go down and wanted me to get a claim to what was mine before he went to jail?"

"I sincerely doubt that those were his intentions." Jakob shook his head. "And at this point, we don't really know what your *rightful* shares are or were."

"What's that supposed to mean?"

"Let me see those papers again." He grabbed them from my hand and read them more carefully this time. "These were signed off by David."

"So?" I was upset at the snark in his voice when he had said *rightful*.

"So why would David sign off on papers giving you a major interest in the company?"

"Maybe he felt guilty as well?" My stomach churned as I spoke. I knew David didn't even have the capacity to feel guilt. And if he did, he didn't go along with a kidnapping to prevent me from getting access to any shares to signing over shares in less than a few weeks.

"Think, Bianca, think. Larry has a daughter, a long-lost daughter, called Roma. Roma came into his life a few years ago. Roma came into my brother's life a few years ago. Roma is *dating* my brother."

"Do you think David knows who Roma is?"

"No." Jakob shook his head. "I don't think he knows there's a connection, but I could be wrong. I mean, this is all larger than I thought it was in the beginning."

"So we need to find Roma now?"

"Hold on." A light went off in his eyes as he stared at me. "Do you have your phone on you?"

"Yes, why?"

"What did Mrs. Renee just say?"

"What? That Larry had a daughter?"

"No, no. I think she gave us a clue." He snapped his fingers. "She made it a point to tell me Larry was the one who chose Mattias's name."

"Yeah, so?"

"She also made a point of saying 'that's my name' right before she left."

"And?" I was confused.

"Give me your phone." He grabbed it from me and typed something in. " 'Reborn'!" he exclaimed.

"What?" I was even more confused than I'd been before.

"*Renee* means 'reborn.' "

"Okay, so?"

"So what if Larry's last name wasn't really Renee?" Jakob grabbed my hand and dragged me to the car with him. "What if he changed his name?"

"To Renee?" I frowned.

"He likes symbolism, so maybe he thought Renee was smart."

"I guess so." I nodded. "I guess it could make sense. He

was reborn as a new person." Then it hit me. I suddenly understood what Jakob was saying. "Are you saying what I think you're saying?"

He nodded. "What if *Larry* was Maxwell?"

"But why would he change his name?"

"That's what we need to find out. He has to be Maxwell, though. It makes the most sense. That's why I always thought he was with the company from the beginning, even though he only started as an attorney when *Maxwell* left." Jakob was about to say something else when my phone started ringing. "Here you go." He looked at the screen as he handed it to me. As soon as he saw the screen, he blanched and the phone fell to the ground as he stared at me in shock.

"What is it?" I bent down and picked up the phone—somehow it had escaped significant damage. I had a missed call from Rosie. "What's wrong?"

"The—the photo on the screen when the phone rang." He stumbled over his words.

"Yeah, I like to do phone indicators in my phone book." I nodded. "So?"

"Do you have any photos of your friend Rosie that I could see larger?" he asked urgently.

"Let me check." I frowned. "Why?"

"Just pull one up," he demanded.

I went to my photo album and opened it quickly. "Here you go." I showed him a photo of Rosie and me at a bar a couple of months ago.

Only his sharp intake of breath betrayed his concern. "Bianca—Rosie *is* Roma."

"What?" I felt the blood drain from my face.

"Bianca, Rosie is David's girlfriend." Jakob paused.

"No." I shook my head. "She can't be. It's not possible."

"Oh, shit, and I think I have something else. I think *Roma* stands for Rosie *Maxwell.* Ro Ma—she takes after her father, likes names to have a significance." He looked at me with intense eyes. "Your best friend, Rosie, is Larry's daughter."

"Oh my God." I stared at Jakob in shock. It all made sense now. Why she'd chosen that bar. Why she'd gone to the bathroom and not had any of the wine. Why she'd so easily believed the bartender when he'd told her I left with a guy. The way she kept bumping into David, even after we broke up. "Shit, she even told me she was working on a deal with Bradley Inc., but she said she didn't get it. Oh my God."

"She must have been working with her dad. That's why the kidnapping plan worked out so perfectly. We had someone on the inside helping out."

"I can't believe she would do this to me."

"Call her back, now." His eyes flared. "Tell her you want to meet her. Don't let her know you know anything."

"Okay." I dialed her number back quickly, fingers trembling. How could Rosie have lied to me? How could she have lied all these years? Was she really working with Larry? Was she really seeing David? My stomach dropped as I thought about the enormity of the lies that could have been going on for years. "She's not answering." I hung up and tried calling back again. "She's not picking up." I clutched the phone tightly.

"Let's go." He glanced back at the house. "Let's get back to the city. I know someone who owes me a favor, and I think we should talk to your friend Blake. Maybe he can check out if there is a connection between Rosie and Larry."

"Should I call him?"

"Yes, call him now. We're going to find out exactly who Rosie is, Bianca, and exactly what role she had in all of this. Give me the envelope." He took it from my hands. "This was definitely a setup. Larry wanted you to stop the merger for reasons that weren't in your best interests."

"What do you think he wanted?" I stared at the envelope in Jakob's hands. "Why would they want me to have shares?"

"There has to be a reason why he wanted to set you up, just like he's set everything else up. He's been playing us, Bianca. He and his daughter have been playing all of us." Jakob frowned. "There is one possible reason why he gave you the shares."

"What's that?"

"Maybe the reason has nothing to do with you getting part of the company. Maybe that was just a cost he had to pay to stop the merger. Maybe he saw you as the only way to get it stopped."

"Couldn't you stop it? Or David?"

"I don't have shares in Bradley Inc.," Jakob said softly.

"It's not my company. My father left all of his shares to David. I told you before that my mother wanted nothing from him."

"Yes, you did tell me that." I stopped talking as I thought. How then had Jakob made so much money? And was he mad that he didn't own part of the corporation? He was Jeremiah's son after all. He should have been left something.

"Larry wanted the merger stopped because he realized that it wouldn't be beneficial to him *and his daughter*," Jakob said. "And perhaps after everything he's done, he just can't accept that it was all for naught."

"I guess his wife was right." I sighed as we drove off. "Larry was evil, Jeremiah was evil . . ." My voice trailed off as I thought about what she'd said. She'd said that all three of them were as bad as each other. The third man was my father.

"We don't know that your dad was bad as well, Bianca." Jakob squeezed my hand.

"Mrs. Renee said they were all bad." Pain rippled through me. "What could my father have done, Jakob? I don't know why or how he could have been involved in all of this."

"It could be a trick, Bianca. Maybe that's the point. Maybe they want you to doubt your father and yourself."

"Why did my dad leave me that letter? What was he hoping I'd figure out?" My voice cracked as my emotions overcame me. "I always thought my parents had the perfect marriage and it was stopped short by my mother's accident.

But what if all that was a lie? What if they never had a perfect love and a perfect life?" I put my face in my hands.

"It'll be okay, Bianca. We'll get to the bottom of everything, I promise you. We won't stop until we have all the answers." Jakob held me close to him, but all I could keep thinking was *Is this something I really want to know?* What had my father been involved with? What had gone on all those years ago between Bradley, London, and Maxwell? Somehow I had a feeling that Rosie was just the tip of the iceberg.

"Hey, Blake, it's me," I said into the phone, trying to sound casual as Jakob drove us back to Manhattan.

"Hey, what's going on?"

"We have more information." I paused. "It's about Rosie."

"Okay." His voice was short at the mention of my friend.

"We think she might be the daughter of the attorney Larry Renee."

"No way!" Blake's voice sounded positively giddy and I frowned.

"That's not something to be happy about."

"I know. I'm sorry."

"We think that Larry Renee is actually Maxwell."

"Maxwell of Bradley, London, and Maxwell?"

"Yes." I could feel Jakob's eyes on me, but I didn't turn to face him. I was confused and upset, and all I wanted was to be alone to think by myself in a hot bath.

"So what do you want me to do?"

"We want you to find any links between Rosie and Larry. Also, see if you can find any connection between Larry and Maxwell."

"And ask him to check out Mrs. Maxwell as well," Jakob intervened. "She obviously seems to have a role if she was threatening Mrs. Renee."

"Yeah, see if you can find out anything about Rosie's mom." I shook my head in annoyance. "I can't believe I never pushed to meet her. We've been friends for all these years, yet I never even really knew who she was."

"You know, I always thought something was off with her," Blake said matter-of-factly. "I don't know why you never saw it."

"There's a lot of things I don't seem to see."

"That's true," Blake said quietly.

I blushed. "So that's it." I made to end the conversation. "Can you check today?"

"Yeah, I'll head out to the library now. Though I think I'll go to NYU's campus."

"You can get into the library without a student ID?"

"I can get in anywhere." He laughed. "Do you want to meet up tonight? Maybe we can discuss what I find over dinner."

"Dinner sounds great." I nodded and heard Jakob clearing his throat. I looked over at him and he had an eyebrow raised. "Jakob and I would love to join you for dinner."

"Great." Blake sounded disappointed. "I'll call you

tonight with a place to meet. And don't worry, Bianca, if there's something to be found, I'll find it."

"Thanks, Blake. And good luck."

"Luck has nothing to do with it." Blake chuckled. "Do you think the Romans had the greatest empire in all of civilization due to luck?"

"I think the Egyptians, the Chinese, the Greeks, and the Mayans would all beg to differ with your statement."

"Touché. I'm sure they would." Blake laughed. "Don't worry, I got this."

"Just be careful."

"Don't worry about me, Bianca. Napoléon once said, 'I am sometimes a fox and sometimes a lion. The whole secret of government lies in knowing when to be the one and when to be the other.' " Blake paused. "And while I may not be a politician, I know how to play many different roles to get the information I need."

"Good luck, my friend. I've missed you and your random quotes."

"I've missed you too, Bianca. I'm glad to be able to help you with this. Stay safe and I'll see you and lover boy at dinner later tonight."

~

I turned to Jakob after I hung up. "I want you to drop me off at my apartment. I want to pick up some of my stuff to take back to your place. I didn't take enough with me."

"That's fine. I'll help you pack."

"No." I shook my head. "I want to take my time, see what I think I'm going to need for the next couple of weeks. I'll be fine. I'll come to your place once I'm done, and then we can go over everything while Blake does his research."

"Take a cab on the way back then. I don't want you taking the subway."

"That's fine."

"Do you have enough money?"

'Yes." I nodded and sighed. I didn't even want to think about money at this point.

"I don't think you should be alone." He sounded annoyed. "But fine, I'll drop you off and wait for you at home."

"Are you going to go straight there?"

"No." He shook his head. "I need to go and see someone first."

"I should come too. Find out what your friend knows."

"I'm not going to see him. We can go and see him tomorrow."

"Are you sure? We can go now if you want and then I can just go to my place tomorrow."

"No, get your stuff now and we'll go and see him later. Tomorrow will be good enough."

"I'm almost scared to hear what Blake finds out." I let out a deep breath. "I'm not sure I can take any more secrets."

"Don't be scared, Bianca. I'm sorry you've been betrayed."

"I just don't know what else I can find out. I just can't believe Rosie is Maxwell's daughter. My father knew Rosie." I sighed. "I don't even know if he knew who she was."

I looked out the window. "I don't even know who I can trust. What I can trust? She's been my friend for years, Jakob."

"We never truly know people, do we?"

"I don't even know if this is real." I glanced at him as I pinched myself. "It doesn't feel real. I don't want it to be real. I want this to be a dream."

"How would we know if this were a dream?" His voice sounded sad. "How do we really know what is real and what can be trusted?"

"We don't." I looked down at my lap as I realized how true my words were. I had no idea who could be trusted. I'd gone back and forth on my feelings toward Jakob. I wanted to believe in him from the depths of my soul, but the more I found out about everything, the more I was losing my faith in humanity.

"I'm glad it's not a dream though." Jakob's voice was firm and he reached out and grabbed my hand. "Even in all this craziness, I'm glad it's not a dream, because if it was a dream, I wouldn't have met you and I wouldn't have you here with me."

"I do believe you just said something romantic to me." I curled my fingers into his. "Who would have thunk it?"

"I can be romantic at times."

"Once in a blue moon, I'm guessing."

"I was pretty romantic on the island, don't you think?"

My mind drifted back to our days in the sun and sand. How far away that seemed now. It was almost like a distant memory in my mind.

"Are you listening, Bianca, or did I scare you?"

"Sorry, what? I didn't hear you?" I looked at him and gave him a weak smile.

"I said, we need to get you that pregnancy test." He looked at me, his eyes blazing. "And if you're pregnant, we should get married."

"What?" I froze in shock.

"I know, that came out wrong. Let's get married anyway. I don't want you to think it's about the baby."

"Oh." My heart was thudding as I gazed at him. I was excited and shocked. I was about to ask him why when my phone beeped and I stared at the text message on the screen in shock.

*It's Steve. We need to talk. Your life is in danger. I told you before to be careful who you fall for. They are all deceiving you. Maybe you'll trust me now. Whatever you do, don't go to David's apartment. Delete this message and wait for my next text. I'm going to help you.*

"Who's that?" Jakob looked over at me with a curious expression.

"It's Steve." I stared into Jakob's eyes in shock. "He says he wants to talk to me. He says my life is in danger and that I should be careful who I fall for. What should I do?"

"Text him back." Jakob's eyes were hard. "Tell him you want to meet up with him."

"When?"

"As soon as possible."

"He told me to wait for him to text me back."

"Then wait. We don't want to give him any reason to disappear again. He could finally provide us some of the answers we've been looking for. He can tell us if he's been working for Larry and what Larry's master plan was. We might have all the answers to all the questions sooner and easier than we thought."

"Yeah, this might all be solved soon." I looked out of the window, my brain not feeling the same hope that was in my voice. "That would be great."

# fourteen

I walked up to my apartment, waited for thirty minutes on the couch, and then left again. I wasn't sure what made me go to David's apartment. Maybe it was because Steve had told me not to go. Maybe I was hoping to catch Rosie and David together. Maybe I just needed that confrontation without Jakob being there. I knew Jakob wouldn't like my going to see David behind his back, but I had bigger concerns than that. I needed to find out where Rosie was and talk to her by myself. I owed that to our friendship. I wanted to confront her alone. I saw Joseph standing at the front of the building and stopped. I didn't want him to alert David that I was coming up to see him.

"Hey, kid," I called out to a small boy eating a large ice cream cone.

"Yeah?" He looked at me warily.

"I need you to go and spill that ice cream on that man." I pointed to Joseph.

"What? For real?" The kid shook his head.

"I'll give you twenty dollars."

"Okay." His eyes lit up as if it were Christmas.

"Here you go." I handed him a twenty and sighed. I should have offered him five. Twenty seemed like an awful lot of money just to dump some ice cream. "Now go." I watched as he ran up to Joseph and threw the cone at his face. Trust me to choose a hooligan. I saw Joseph chasing down the kid and I walked quickly to the building, avoiding looking in their direction as I hurried into the building. My heart was beating fast as I made my way into the elevator. I'd made it. I exited the elevator quickly and hurried to David's apartment. I tried opening the door without knocking. I grinned as it opened easily. He needed to get his locks fixed. The bottom lock never locked the door unless it was slammed it hard. I crept inside the apartment and froze as I heard two voices coming from the study. I walked slowly and crept up to the door that was slightly ajar and peeked in. But no one was there.

"What are you going to do, Jakob?" David's voice said clearly, and I froze.

"I'm still deciding," Jakob responded gruffly.

I looked around the room in confusion. Where were the noises coming from? No one was in the room. Then I saw the small AM/FM transistor radio sitting on the floor next to the desk. I crouched down and picked it up—the sounds were coming from there.

"You're a fool, you know that, right?" David's voice was

full of static as I held the radio to my ear. Where were they? I hurried out of the study and looked around the rest of the apartment quickly.

Beep beep. I grabbed my phone to see who had texted me.

*Smart girl. It's Steve again. I'm glad you went to David's apartment. Go to the TV in his bedroom. Turn it to channel 1003 now. I told you to trust me.*

*How do you know where I am?*

*Don't worry about that. Go to the TV in David's room now.*

*What's going on?* I texted back as I ran into David's room and turned the TV on.

*All will be revealed in due time.*

*Where is Jakob?* I asked, my heart pounding as I fumbled with the numbers on the remote and changed the channel to 1003.

*You'll see.* Steve texted back immediately.

I sighed at the message and then looked at the TV screen. My heart dropped as I saw Jakob and David in a dark, dingy room somewhere. Jakob, with a grimace on his face, was standing next to David, who was tied to a chair and looked panicked.

"The papers were at Larry's wife's house, just like she said." Jakob's voice was cold. "You didn't tell me she was Larry's daughter."

"I didn't know at first." David's voice was bitter. "Not until you were on the island."

"You know Larry is Maxwell?"

"What?" David's jaw dropped. "That bitch never told me!"

"Don't worry. I'll take care of her." Jakob walked to the side of the room and I could barely see him in the darkness.

"You got what you wanted. You can't keep me here," David grunted. "You won't get away with it."

"It's nearly done now." Jakob slammed his hand down on the table. "Everything is working out perfectly. I've done what I had to do. What's hers is mine and what is mine will be hers."

"What do you think she'll do when she finds out?" David's voice was low and he smirked at Jakob from his seat. "You've got me tied up here so I can't leave, but you'll have to let me loose at some point."

"We'll see about that." Jakob's voice dropped to a low rasp and I shivered. "I might never let you loose."

"Bianca will find out, you know." David sounded scared now. "She'll find out the truth." My heart stopped as I watched them both. What truth was David talking about?

"What truth is that, dear brother?"

"She'll find out that the kidnapping was your idea." David's voice cracked as he struggled in his seat. I could see the tightness of the rope around his wrists and I felt my own wrists scratching as I remembered the feeling.

"Why would she find that out?"

"I think it would make a big difference to her to know I wasn't the mastermind behind the kidnapping. When she finds out it was all your idea. Did you like tying the rope around her body and her wrists?" David hissed. "You're a sick fuck, aren't you? I know she has a cute little—"

"Shut up." Jakob slapped David across the face and I gasped. I was starting to feel woozy from watching the screen and took a step back.

"Or what? You're going to kill me?" David laughed. "Killing me won't stop the truth from emerging. Wait until she finds out that it was you who wanted her out of the way. Wait until she finds out that it was *your* company that bought Bradley Inc. That it's you who doesn't want her stopping the merger."

"That kills you, doesn't it, baby brother?"

"You were always jealous of me and what I had." David spat at him. "I had everything that you wanted. I even had her."

"You never had her."

"That's what she likes to say, but I fucked her in every hole she has and she loved it. She was begging me for more when I had her in the bed."

"You sick fuck." Jakob slapped him again and David laughed.

"She'll never trust you, you know. Not now and not ever. Not when she finds out exactly what you did. Not when she finds out why."

"What are you talking about?" Jakob's voice went cold as ice. As did my face as I took a few steps closer to the TV screen.

"I'm talking about her father."

"What?" Jakob grabbed hold of David's shirt. "Think very carefully before you speak next, little brother."

"I'm talking about your whore of a mother and Bianca's father." David laughed. "Does Bianca know that her precious father was the one cheating?"

Jakob stood there still as a statue and my hand flew to my mouth to stifle a gasp. All of a sudden my father's grief made a lot more sense. Larry's wife had been right. They'd all been evil.

"And not only that . . ." David's eyes narrowed. "Does Bianca know exactly what happened to her father? I think she'd be interested in finding out more about his *death*. Don't you?"

"What do you know about her father's death?" Jakob tightened his hold on David's shirt.

"I spoke to Larry, who spoke to Steve. I know who Steve was working for," David spat out, and then smiled a wide, evil smile. "And all hell's about to break loose, dear brother."

"You spoke to Larry?" Jakob's voice dropped. "If you want any chance of getting out of here, you better tell me what game he's playing."

"Death was just the beginning," David said slowly, and I froze at the familiar words. "You've been a bad, bad boy, Jakob."

"What does that mean?"

"You thought the target of everything was Bianca." David laughed. "But you were wrong. The target has been you, all along."

"What?"

"It's game, set, and match, Jakob. You're going to lose everything. Once Bianca knows the truth about what you've done, it will be all over for you." David laughed. "It will be all over."

The screen went blank and I stared at the black and gray lines, my mind buzzing. What the fuck was going on?

Beep beep. I grabbed my phone, expecting another text from Steve. I needed to see him right away. I needed to find out what he knew. I clutched my head and rubbed my temple as I felt a huge migraine hit me.

*Bianca, we need to talk now.* Blake's name flashed on the screen. *You and Jakob need to come and meet up with me. I think you've both been set up.*

I was about to call Blake when I heard the door behind me closing.

"It's me, Bianca," said the familiar voice. "I'm here."

I turned around and took one look at the person in front of me before the world turned as black as it had the day I learned my father had died. I fainted clean away.

Keep reading for a sneak peek at the next installment in the tantalizing, heart-stopping Swept Away series by *New York Times* bestselling author J.S. Cooper

# Resolution

Coming Summer 2015 from Gallery Books!

# prologue

"Hush, little baby, don't say a fucking word," he sang in an ominous voice as he twisted the lyrics to the old nursery rhyme. His voice was the only sound in the small damp space aside from a low rattling in the corner, and I didn't want to know what or who was making that noise.

I kept my face stiff and my eyes downward as I sat there uncomfortably. The room was cold and dark and smelled of mold. I coughed as the mildew filled my lungs and my body shivered on the old rickety chair I was tied to. I didn't even bother trying to scream—I knew no one would hear me. No one would be coming to my rescue now. It was just the two of us. After everything, it had come to this.

My head dropped forward as I grew tired. I just wanted to sleep. I wanted to sleep and forget that any of this had ever happened, not because I was scared of this moment but because my heart ached for all the moments of the last week, for the devastating truth that I'd had to accept. It wasn't about fear of the man in front of me—but I couldn't even look at him without feeling a gamut of emotions from heartache to guilt. This moment was poetic justice; the weaving paths of our forefathers had led us inevitably here. I knew there was nothing either of us could say or do to change the direction our paths had led us down.

"I didn't want everything to go like this." He held the gun to my head. "You understand that, right? I don't want to hurt you. I didn't want it to come to this."

I nodded my understanding, my throat too constricted to speak. My body was frozen in fear as an image of a black stallion running down a white sandy beach flashed into my mind. I'm not sure where the image came from, but somehow it calmed me.

"A life for a life, right?" His voice sounded broken and raw. "That's what they say." His voice echoed his sorrow. I could tell he thought he had no other option. I couldn't allow myself to look up at him. All I could think was, *Is this how it's all going to end for me?*

"He shouldn't have done that to my parents, Bianca." His voice was pained. "He ruined my life."

"I understand," I said softly, my voice cracking as I spoke. I *did* understand. I didn't know if I could blame him. "It's not your fault."

"You're making this hard for me, Bianca." He sighed and moved the gun away from my head, kneeling down next to my chair. He grabbed my chin and forced me to look at him. His eyes gazed into mine and I could see the regret shining at me. Regret, and another emotion I recognized. My heart thudded as I stared back at him. I still had a shot at changing my story. The emotion in his eyes was one I knew well. It was a gaze of adoration. He still had feelings for me. That was the opening I needed to try and change his mind.

"You don't have to do this," I said softly. "You don't have to go through with it."

"I do," he said, but his voice was unsure as he gazed at me, his eyes scrutinizing my face.

"No. If you do this, we can't be together." I nearly choked on the words, but I had to say them. It was my only chance.

"You would want to be with me?" He froze. "After all this?"

"Yes." I nodded and made myself smile. "We're meant to be together, don't you see that?"

"It was always you, you know." His fingers touched my leg. "From the first time I saw you, I knew."

"So then don't do this!" I pleaded with him. "This doesn't have to be the end for us. This can be the beginning!"

"A new beginning?" He spoke softly, his eyes glazing over as he considered what I'd said.

"Maybe this is why everything happened," I said, almost choking on my words. "Maybe we're meant to be together. Maybe this was fate's cruel joke on us. Maybe this was the only way we could be together."

"Maybe." He nodded and stepped back. My body was trembling as I waited for him to decide what he was going to do next. “You really think we’re soul mates?” He stared at my lips and it took everything in me not to shudder. And then, suddenly, there was a loud bang. I screamed. He fell forward, his head hitting my lap hard, and I screamed again.

“No!” I could feel tears falling from my eyes as blood, red and sticky, pooled in my lap. “Nooo!” I screamed, looking into his face. What had just happened? I wasn’t even sure. He gazed at me with a weak smile, the life draining from his face.

“Your father did this to us,” he mumbled. “He did this to me . . .”

“No,” I whispered, my stomach churning as I felt a wave of arctic coldness fill me. “I’m sorry.” I meant it. This wasn’t how it was supposed to end.

“Hush, little baby, don’t say a fucking word.” This time his voice was but a whisper in the coldness. “This is how it should be.”